Finding Freedom

Book Four of the Piper Anderson Series

Danielle Stewart

Copyright Page

ISBN-13: 978-1496014337

Cover Art by: Ginny Gallagher
Website: Ginsbooknotes

Dedication

This book is dedicated to the readers who have embraced the Piper Anderson Series. If you've enjoyed these books it means you believe there is always hope, and you are never truly alone.

Jedda

I killed my parents. I looked down at them as they lay asleep in their bed. I drew in a steadying breath and filled my nose with the stale air of the small apartment bedroom. The stench of neglect, fear, and abuse fueled my resolve. Squeezing my eyes shut, I pulled the trigger—once, twice. The pops were louder than I thought they would be, and my ears rang as the echo of my crime reverberated off the walls. I felt the warm spray of blood as it mixed with the sweat on my face. With my eyes still closed tightly, I continued to grip the gun fiercely as my whole body began to shake. With my back leaning against the wall for support, I slowly lowered myself to the floor to wait for the police to come. Despite my physical reaction to what I had just done, I felt an eerie calmness inside me.

It was a long road that led me to that moment, and I didn't travel it alone. Just a room away from the gunpowder and death, at a mere eight years old, was my little sister, Willow. She was the personification of her name: slight, soft, and yielding. I prayed that deep down she had the strength and resilience that also described her namesake. Could she bend to the winds that were trying to blow us over?

Years before I shot my parents I remember sitting with Willow. We were holding hands on a hard wooden bench outside a government office and overheard how our lives would change. All parental rights were severed. Our mother was given probation. Our father was to serve eight months in prison. That wasn't even a month for each scar I had on my body as a result of his cruelty. Before I could fully process the injustice of that small sentence, I was met with another blow. Willow and I were separated, quickly ushered away to different foster families.

As I met my new family, the Wrights, I was already silently planning my escape from them. My damaged heart fought to reject the sincerity that was shown to me by my foster parents and foster brother, Bobby. Slowly though, without realizing it, I softened. I was so hungry for love and attention that I stopped fighting it and I became part of the Wright family. And, no, the irony of their name didn't escape me, even as a young boy. I knew the Wrights were right for me.

In the process of becoming part of their family I let my little heart slip away from my sister. Nearly two years went by before I found out, far too late, that because of some kind of glitch in the paperwork, she'd been placed back with our parents. Driven by half-buried instincts, I found her, and that image changed my life forever. I saw her chained to a radiator, lying on a mattress that smelled like death. Her half-starved body wore the marks of hideous abuse, burns and scars etched across her small limbs. I don't think I really knew what I was feeling at the time; the burning sensation I first felt the day Willow and I were separated was spreading with an intensity I'd never known.

Three weeks after finding her in that horrific state I sat shaking on the floor of my parents' bedroom listening to the wailing of police sirens growing closer and closer. It was worth it. I was ready to face my crime. As long as Willow was safe, I didn't care what happened to me.

Chapter One

"Do you have any questions for me?" the mousy victim's advocate, Delma, in her much too large business suit, asked as she looked expectantly over at Jedda. He was staring down at the pile of clothes in front of him as though he was looking at some kind of Holy Grail. He was lost in the lines and seams of the fabric, the crispness of the denim.

The conference room they sat in was one normally used for lawyers and clients to discuss their case. When he'd entered a few minutes earlier he'd taken inventory of the nearly empty room: three chairs, a sterile looking metal table, and two-way glass across the far wall. A guard outside the door. It was nothing special, but after sixteen years in prison any change of scenery was welcomed. Even a mundane, nearly empty room.

"No questions at all?" the woman asked again, her impatient tone shaking Jedda from the spell he was under.

"I'm not s-s-sure," he stuttered out, looking over at Michael for direction. "I'm not really sure what to ask."

"Well," Delma hummed out, seeming slightly annoyed, "you've been incarcerated for sixteen years. Going out in to society is not a simple transition."

"He's going to have a great support system," Michael chimed in and shook his head reassuringly back at Jedda. "He'll do great."

"In another situation, Mr. Cooper, I'd say your optimism is refreshing, but in this case I'm going to caution you against it. We're talking about someone who was put in prison at the age of fifteen for committing a double homicide. He's had no social development. No formal schooling past that age. You know as well as I do that the technology developed in the last ten years alone would be enough to make someone feel completely overwhelmed. He'll struggle to find employment, considering he isn't being exonerated, only paroled early. This will always be on his record. Now, I see he has a younger sister who's attending a music school here in New York. I don't imagine she'll have the means to support him emotionally or financially." Throughout her speech the woman's arms remained crossed over her chest with an air of superiority.

"I petitioned the court for Jedda to come back to Edenville, North Carolina, with me. We received word yesterday that he'll be able to."

"Mr. Cooper." The smug grimace on her face was enough to infuriate anyone, but Jedda was steering clear of the tension in the room. He pushed his lips tightly closed and listened as she continued. "I didn't peg you for a bleeding heart attorney taking in strays. You actually think you're in a position to help him? I'd imagine the only reason the court allowed it is to make him some other state's problem."

"What is your deal?" Michael snapped, narrowing his eyes at her. "You're a victim's advocate. If anyone is supposed to have a bleeding heart, it should be you."

"The key word there is victim's advocate. Normally I'd be sitting here with the family of the people murdered. I'd be comforting a person who'd been attacked or someone who'd been exploited. This is the first time I've been assigned to a murderer. I don't really agree with what's transpired here. He was sentenced to life without parole."

Jedda watched as Michael stiffened his back and narrowed his eyes at Delma. "Well then, it's a damn good thing it's not your place to agree or disagree. Your role is to offer support to whoever's case you're assigned, and if you can't for some reason, then you should recuse yourself."

"Trust me, Mr. Cooper, I tried. No one else in my office was willing to take the case. No one felt he should be let free. He killed his mother and father."

"He killed two sex-trafficking abusive monsters who were on the verge of selling his younger sister. She'd have been gone for good into a dark world I'd imagine you know a lot about, considering your job. He'd seen the police in and out of his house, facilitating the workings of the trafficking ring. He'd been surrounded by violence and had seen how snitches were punished. How can you expect him to have found someone he could trust? After he committed the murders, he immediately pleaded guilty and never spoke a word about why he did it."

"Exactly, and for that he received a life sentence. He could have had a trial and let the evidence fall where it may. It's not society's problem that he chose to not say a word about why he killed them."

"He didn't speak up because he was trying to give his sister a chance at a decent life. One that didn't include her being dragged through a trial. He wanted his adoptive parents to be left alone, free from retribution or harm. He took this sentence like a burden he had to carry alone. He was a kid. Staying quiet was the wrong choice but he did it for the right reasons. Did you miss the parade of prison guards and staff in there with glowing accounts of the kind of inmate Jedda was? He didn't have a single infraction while behind bars which is almost unheard of. He's gotten his GED for God's sake. If he'd had a good lawyer, if there was a trial, he likely wouldn't have been convicted, and if he was, his sentence would have been greatly reduced. Obviously I'm right since the court agreed."

"Fabulous. We all know how infallible the court system is. They must have gotten it right, this time." The woman slammed shut her notebook and crammed it firmly into her briefcase. She continued to mutter something about how Jedda would likely do it again.

"You know what?" Michael cut in with an odd look on his face. "I'm glad we had you here today. It's great practice for the ignorance we're likely to face. So while you served absolutely no other purpose today, just know you earned your paycheck in some ass backward way. But as a victim's advocate you're about as useful as an inflatable dart board."

Jedda's eyes had grown wide and he could feel the electric energy buzzing through the room. He wasn't saying a word. Making waves at this point would be crazy, he could practically taste the fresh air, feel the sun on his face. Pissing anyone off when he was so close to freedom would be foolish.

An exasperated huff escaped the woman's thin and pursed lips as she yanked open the door to the conference room. The blur of her tan oversized suit was all Jedda saw as she stormed away.

Jedda still kept his lips sealed as Michael stood up and took a lap around the room. "Sorry, that got a little intense," he apologized as he paced in frustration.

"Michael, you never have to apologize to me for anything. You've given me my life back." He hesitated and sucked in his bottom lip, then let it out, unable to hold in his laugh. "An inflatable dart board?"

"I've been spending way too much time with Betty. You'll see soon enough. It's like learning a second language. Plus you've said thank you so many times already, Jedda, please, it's my pleasure."

"And you've said that so many times, but you haven't told me why. You've only known Bobby for almost a year. Why do all this for him? You've put your whole life on hold."

"Some relationships are about quality, not quantity, of time. That's the case for Bobby and me. He introduced me to my future wife and mother of my soon-to-be child. He's always had my back."

"Still, that doesn't seem enough. You've moved your wedding day back twice. Won't Jules want to wring your neck?"

"The funny thing about Jules is she'd whoop my ass for leaving my socks hanging around, but this stuff she understands. Well, she has up until this point. She's about a month from her due date and all she wants is to be married before she goes into labor. She said she's holding that little girl in until we've said 'I do.' You and I are flying out in the morning so we'll be back in plenty of time to pull off a wedding."

"Flying?" Jedda's face grew hot, and sweat began to bead across his back.

"Yes, we need to be at the airport early. I've got all our paperwork ready and we've got clearance from the court. When you're ready we'll get out of here. You're free to go."

Jedda reached down and ran his thumb over the seam of the jeans sitting in front of him. "Do you know how weird it is to have these clothes here?"

"I'm sorry if they're not your style. I didn't have much time to shop this morning. They should fit though, and we can buy you something else when we get to Edenville."

"No, they're perfect. I just mean that it's been so long since I've worn actual clothes. I've been in prison orange since I was fifteen years old. Getting these clothes, it just . . ." Jedda swallowed back his emotions as he pulled the green sweatshirt against his chest.

At the feel of Michael's hand clamping down on his shoulder, Jedda pulled in a deep breath. Michael's grip on him was grounding, exactly what he needed at that moment. "I've never flown before," Jedda managed to mutter as he stood.

"You'll be the second person this year I've had to fly with who wasn't quite ready. I've got a sneaking suspicion you'll be better at it than Betty was. I'll let you change. I'll be right outside the door." Michael's small smile was the first Jedda had seen from him. Up until this point it had been all business. His voice was softer now as he reminded Jedda, "You're about to walk out of here a free man."

"I'm not sure I'll be able to walk. My legs are shaking."

"You've got this," Michael assured him as he stepped outside of the small room. "You're going to do great."

Chapter Two

The flight was more redemptive than terrifying. Not by much, but enough to help Jedda get through it. There was something therapeutic about ascending into the sky, away from the darkest place he'd ever been. The clouds were like a protective blanket, wrapping around him. No one could get him up here. His ever-present fear that this was all a big mistake and he'd be thrown back in jail was like a ghost that followed him around, constantly whispering doubt in his ear. But up in the sky, the humming of the plane engine seemed to drown the worry.

His mind rambled through the last two months and how he'd ended up here, flying through the wide-open sky as a free man. It was easy to remember everyone who'd spoken out against him. All the people who wrote him angry letters or fought to keep him in prison. But there was someone he was trying to forget who kept creeping to the forefront of his mind.

Crystal Wardyga was the only person who'd shown even the slightest bit of kindness toward Michael and Jedda while they worked on his case. During the preparation for Jedda's court appearances, Michael was a near constant presence at the prison and courthouse. Jedda still remembered the morning Michael relayed the story of his meeting Crystal, a courtroom stenographer. Michael had spilled a full cup of coffee on himself and was trying to pat it dry when she came into the hallway. She'd directed him to the lost and found, a good place to shop for a new shirt in a pinch. When Michael told Crystal about Jedda and what they were trying to accomplish she listened intently. Soon she was coming to see Jedda during visiting hours and doing what she could to help them both. Often it was just pointing them in the right direction or warning them about people to avoid if possible. She knew the politics and drama of this courthouse, and it helped them tremendously.

At some point, she became personally invested in Jedda's freedom. The more details that came out about the circumstances of his crime, the more she believed he should go free.

Though he frequently missed social cues, Crystal's kindness was not lost on Jedda. The softness in her blue eyes was comforting on days when he felt nothing could calm him. Her visits were flooded with blind optimism. Her belief in his freedom was the only thing that carried him through some days. Michael was there out of friendship for Bobby, and although he and Jedda had certainly grown close, Crystal was something different. She didn't have to be there, she chose to visit. She chose to help.

Saying goodbye to her was harder than Jedda had expected. He could still smell her jasmine perfume on the collar of his shirt. They hadn't talked about what it would look like once he actually was free. She knew they were going to petition the court for Jedda to be allowed to go to Edenville with Michael, but no one knew if it would be approved. When it was, Crystal and Jedda realized it might be the end of the road for their friendship. She tried to talk about the future but he avoided it.

The tears that had gathered in the corner of her ocean blue eyes never fell. She held them, pushed them back, and managed a smile. So he did the same. He certainly wasn't in the position to start a relationship with anyone. In reality, no matter how attracted to her he was, the forced distance might be the best thing that ever happened to her.

As the flight landed, the bumping of the tires gripping the runways and the whining of the engine as it ground to a stop was exactly how Jedda's heart was feeling. Touching back down to reality with a thud, a tug, and a jolt.

Jedda realized watching Michael was a strange experience. He'd never known anyone like him. Michael knew which twists and turns would lead to the airport parking garage. He confidently navigated the construction-filled roads leading to the highway. No sweat on his brow, no nerves at all. He knew who should get a tip and how much. Casual conversation with the other passengers about politics or the state of things came completely naturally to him. He knew himself, he knew the world, and he knew the rules. Jedda wondered if he'd ever be like that, or if he'd always walk through life feeling unsure of himself. A little left behind. He and Michael were around the same age, but to Jedda they felt worlds apart in ability.

"Everything is so different," Jedda said, running his hand across the shiny sleek interior of Michael's car. "How do you have so many radio stations? Is this a talk radio station dedicated just to baseball?"

"Yes. It's satellite radio. It's kind of nuts how many stations there are. Something for everyone really."

"And earlier you sent a message to Jules just by talking it into your phone? Is it like a recording?"

"It converts it to a text message that shows up on her phone," Michael said, handing his smart phone over to Jedda. "You can mess around with it if you want. There's the Internet on there. I have a bunch of apps too."

"Apps, like appetizers. Like recipes?" Jedda asked, looking quizzically down at the small screen.

"No," Michael chuckled, "it's short for applications. There's an app for everything. I can check the stock market, see what movies are playing at every theater within a hundred miles, and buy tickets right from my phone. Download books instantly. Video chat. Watch movies. Do my banking. I don't know how I ever lived without one. Everyone's got one these days."

"A lot of this is allowed in prison now, but you have to have the money and the family on the outside willing to get you set up. The Wrights offered last year to get me some device that would let me send emails, but I told them I was all set. I didn't want to put them out and I wasn't sure I could even learn any of it. I preferred to just read any book I could get my hands on."

"You probably made the right choice. I can't remember the last book I read, like paper in my hands. I read on a device now. I'm sure you would have picked it up quickly though. I can't believe what I've learned to do with this stuff but it's really very distracting.

"I noticed. It seemed like everyone in the airport was fiddling around with one. They looked a little like zombies. I saw a guy walk straight into the ladies room while looking down at his phone. How long has it been like that? People zoned out on technology?"

"Good question. A couple years now I guess. You won't see them at Betty's house. She's a stickler for good old-fashioned conversation. I sneak away to the bathroom to check my email every now and then but she gives me a look like she's onto me."

"I'm looking forward to meeting her. And seeing Bobby. He's doing good, right? You said he's engaged to someone and they're good for each other?"

"Engaged is a term we use loosely with those two. It's really a running joke with all of us. He slipped a ring on her finger when she was just out of major surgery and was still heavily medicated. We give him a hard time about how he took the easy way out and didn't have to say all the mushy stuff the rest of us guys do. It drives him nuts. Piper's a good sport about it but even she gives him a hard time. They are great together. He's a bit of a perfectionist and she likes to push the boundaries. They balance each other perfectly. He's really looking forward to having you down here. Are you still feeling good about everything?"

"I kind of feel like I'm on overload. So many things have changed out here. It feels like I'm on another planet, but I'm sure I'll get used to it eventually." The nervous shake in Jedda's leg felt completely out of his control. He was antsy, and that rhythmic tapping and shaking of his foot was all that kept him from reaching for the car door handle and jumping out.

Michael tapped the button on his steering wheel that turned off the radio. "So I asked everyone to let you get settled in. I don't want you overwhelmed when you first get here."

"Thanks," Jedda said, craning his neck to catch another glimpse at the dozen miniature ponies they just passed. He'd never been in the country before.

"You didn't let me finish," Michael said with an odd smile. "No one actually gives a crap what I say. So I'm imagining they all decided they knew what's best and they'll be at Betty's ready to welcome you. It takes some getting used to, all the attention. I didn't live that way before I met all of them, but they eventually beat you into submission and make you love it. I won't lie, at the beginning, they seem crazy."

"Really?" Jedda asked, trying to determine what level of crazy Michael might be referring to. Was he using it in the casual sense or were these people actually insane? The question dancing in his head must have shown on his face because Michael quickly corrected himself.

"They are unique. Not crazy. I promise you will get used to it, then one day you'll wake up and wonder how the hell you made it all these years without someone in your face reminding you how much they love you, or telling you how stupid something you are about to do is. You start to wonder how you ever survived on your own. It's this weird soul-deep kind of love. God, listen to me, I even sound like them now."

Jedda nodded, trying to act as though he wasn't intimidated by the idea of what waited for him at the end of this ride. "It's nice here," he thought out loud as he turned his body in the front seat of the car to get a better look at the world passing by him. Sprawling patches of grass, fences that seemed to go on forever.

"Edenville also takes some adjusting to. I think it will be a good fit for you. Half the technology and changes that have happened to the world, all the things you've missed, still haven't come to Edenville. It's a nice slow pace."

"What brought a guy like you down here? You seem to fit better in New York."

"That's a long story for another day. How I got to Edenville is tricky, but why I stayed is about to become abundantly clear to you. Betty's house is right up here."

Jedda twisted the string on the hood of his sweatshirt around his finger nervously. He held his breath and let the tightness around his finger take all of his attention.

"I'm scared out of my mind," he muttered as he closed his eyes. His heart was racing, thudding against his ribs. His hands felt tingly and his mouth was painfully dry.

"Everyone here is in your corner, Jedda. I promise."

"I'm not worried about that. I'm terrified I'm going to let them down. I know it sounds like a no-brainer, getting out of prison, but that place was all I've known for half my life. There's structure in there. I knew what every day would be like. Now I have no idea what I'm doing five minutes from now. What if I can't hack it out here? What if letting me out was a mistake?"

"I don't know the answer to that," Michael admitted as Betty's house came into view. "All I know is if I were in your shoes this is where I would want to be. This place, and these people, this is your best shot."

Jedda pried his eyes open and shook his head in agreement, trying to convince himself that Michael was right. He let his eyes focus on the long dirt driveway. The house was surrounded on three sides by tall trees that looked like ancient sentinels keeping watch over everything. There was a stone wall lining the driveway, and Jedda watched as squirrels danced in and out of the holes in it. The house wasn't like any he'd seen up close. He was more accustomed to high-rises. This one reminded him of something he'd watched on the old black and white movies that used to run on basic television when he was a kid. It was country, and seemed completely welcoming, just as Michael had assured him.

Judging by the cars lined up next to the house, Michael's request for a quiet arrival had indeed been ignored. As they pulled in, Jedda felt the sweat begin to bead on the back of his neck and forehead. New people. New place. New life. He should feel like the luckiest man in the world, but in reality, he felt like everything was spinning out of control.

He and Michael stepped up the creaky front porch steps and were greeted by an older woman wearing a pink flowered dress and an apron. Her caramel-colored hair was streaked with gray, and her smile was as warm and sincere as anything Jedda had ever seen. She was small in stature but stood with a stance that said, "Watch out, I am deceivingly formidable."

"Jedda, we're so happy to have you here," she sang in a southern drawl as she stepped aside for Michael and Jedda to pass her. Michael leaned in and kissed her cheek as she patted his back. Again, Jedda froze. Was he supposed to kiss her cheek, too? Was that what everyone did or just what Michael did? Before he could get too lost in his own insecurity, Betty was pulling him into a tight hug and patting his back affectionately.

"What a journey you've been on," she whispered to him as she let him go. Jedda hadn't had a lot of hugs in his life and especially from someone he just met. But the rumors were true, he could see it already. There was something different about this woman. Something indescribably distinct. Sometimes it's not about the expression on someone's face as they look at you, it's about how they see you. That's all Jedda could think as he took in the woman who'd thrown her arms around a killer without a moment's hesitation. She was seeing him in a way he hadn't been seen for a very long time. It felt like she was looking at the boy he used to be rather than the man who'd made some taken lives.

"I'm Betty. I'm sure you've heard loads of wonderful things about me. They're all true." The kitchen and small breakfast area was full of people and uncomfortable silence. The only one ignoring that air in the room was Betty. She might as well be wielding a knife and cutting right through the awkwardness. "I'll do the introductions. This here is my daughter, Jules, and she's carrying my granddaughter who, if my daughter loves me at all, will be named Françoise after my grandmother."

"Ma, I thought we put that to rest already," the red-headed beauty with the beach-ball belly said as she rolled her eyes and perched her hands on her hips. "She'll be the only kid in kindergarten with an old lady name." After some huffing and puffing passed between Jules and Betty the attention turned back to Jedda. "Sorry about that, Jedda. Ma thinks she knows what's best for everyone all the time," Jules said as she extended her hand and smiled warmly at him. "You'll see."

"Don't go warning the boy about me like I'm not standing right here." More knowing looks passed between the women while Jedda tried to keep up with what was good-hearted humor and what was real tension.

When everyone was quiet again, Jedda stuttered for the words he'd rehearsed over and over again in his head on the plane ride. He had a message for Jules and hoped it would come out halfway normal. "Thank you for allowing Michael to be away as long as he was. I know you bought a house and even put off your wedding twice. I'm very grateful."

"It's me who should be thanking you," she replied in her heavy southern drawl as she looked over Jedda's shoulder and narrowed her eyes at Michael. "You see my fiancé here is a whiz-bang of a lawyer as I'm sure you were witness to. He's charismatic, knows the law books inside and out. Impressive really."

"Yes," Jedda said, nodding his head in agreement, but before his lips could curl into a smile Jules changed her tone.

"Now here at home is another story all together. Here he's a moron. You keeping him up there is probably what's allowed me to stay engaged to him."

Jedda pursed his lips shut and leaned over slightly to the side so that Jules's dagger-filled eyes were able to reach Michael better.

"I said I was sorry a dozen times already. You're being too sensitive."

"Too sensitive," Jules crowed as she charged forward, pushing Jedda aside slightly. "You called your very pregnant wife fat. I don't think people would consider me too sensitive."

"It was almost a month ago and I did not call you fat. I said that I hadn't seen you in a few weeks and you were bigger than I thought you would be."

The whole room drew in a tight breath as though they'd just witnessed a horrible unavoidable accident with lots of carnage.

Jules's jaw fell open as she shook her head in disbelief. "I can't believe you just repeated that. I swear to God, Michael Cooper, I will make you pray for death if you don't shut your mouth and—"

"Jules," Betty said softly, resting her hand on her daughter's shoulder. "Please punish the idiot later. You're scaring our company. Now where was I?" Betty turned to a man in the corner of the room. "This is Clay. He's my companion. He's from up in New York just like you. He's a chef and moved down to Edenville to start up a restaurant with me. It's always been a dream of mine and I know with his help it will come true." Betty swooned as she rested her hand on Clay's shoulder and grinned.

The stout balding man tipped his head in greeting and went back to busying himself with the corn he'd been husking. "We're happy to have you here, Jedda, and I'm extra happy about it because it means I'm not the new guy in the house anymore. Make yourself at home here."

Betty leaned in and kissed Clay's cheek affectionately before she continued. "You of course, already know Bobby," Betty said as Bobby sprang forward and pulled Jedda into a tight hug, their bodies thudding together.

"This place comes with built-in commotion, so I thought I'd give you a minute before I rushed you," Bobby said, slapping Jedda's shoulder and looking at him again as though he couldn't believe he was actually here. "Congratulations, Jedda. I'm so happy you're out. It took all my willpower not to tackle you when you came in the door, but I didn't want to interrupt Michael getting his ass handed to him by Jules."

"I can't thank you enough for what you've done for me, Bobby. What you're all willing to do for me. I'm not sure how I'll ever pay you back but I—"

"For the love of Pete, Bobby, you brought us another one? Jedda, my boy, sit down here." Betty gestured to a chair at the breakfast nook and shooed Bobby out of her way.

"Another what?" Bobby asked, looking confused as to why he'd been shoved aside.

"Now listen here, Jedda. I'm not going to make the same mistake twice. When we met Piper over there I wasn't as direct as I needed to be."

Michael let out a burst of air as he interrupted, "Yes, that's what you're known for Betty. Not being direct enough." He had to duck to avoid the dishtowel Betty resolutely tossed at his face.

"You best hush your mouth or I won't save you from her next time," she threatened with a nod toward Jules. "Now, as I was saying, I know you won't really hear this when I tell you, but I'm going to say it anyway right from the get-go. You aren't here because we owe Bobby some debt. Trust me, that boy owes me more than he can ever pay back. You aren't here because we're a bunch of big-hearted charitable do-gooders. You're here because you're a part of this. Someone we care about cares about you. You belong here and you don't owe us anything. I know that won't sink in right now. Every other word out of your mouth will be I'm sorry or thank you. But you need to know the sooner you realize you deserve to be here, the better off you'll be."

Jedda hung his head and let his eyes fix on his brand new white shoes. Betty was right, he wasn't ready to believe that, but it was still nice to hear. "Can I ask you something?" He was still looking down and speaking just above a whisper.

"Anything," Betty said crouching down slightly to meet his eye.

"What smells so good?" His head rose and a smile broke across his face. Jedda loved food. Cooking was one of the only real freedoms he'd had in prison and as hard as he tried to decipher what Betty might have in the oven, he just couldn't figure it out.

The woman who'd been sitting next to Bobby smiled and answered his question. "She didn't know what you liked so she made one of everything. Italian food, southern food, French. She wanted to be sure there was something here you'd enjoy. That's just how she is," she said as she stepped forward and put her arm around Betty. "It's nice to meet you, Jedda. I'm Piper. You're a very important part of Bobby's life. That means you're important to the rest of us. We're glad to have you here and we'll help you any way we can."

Piper was not at all what Jedda had expected. The way she'd been described by Michael and Bobby, you'd think she was this fierce ball of terror, plowing her way through life, kicking ass and taking names. But she seemed pretty normal. Though there was a flash of something in her eyes. A kind of knowing. He'd gotten the short version of what Piper had lived through, but looking at her now made him want to hear more. He wanted to understand her better because there was a chance she might be more like him than any of the others in the group. And if she could be this happy, then there might be hope for him after all.

One thing was already abundantly clear. The meal was truly a smorgasbord of different types of food, each one delicious. Pasta. Pot pie. Grits. And so much more. An endless buffet lined up on the kitchen counter for everyone to enjoy. The food was good, but the company was even better. It was a stark contrast to eating in the chow hall. That was where the politics of prison played out—the drama and the danger. You ate quickly and left even quicker. This meal was relaxing, fun even. He didn't have to look over his shoulder or shovel his food so fast that he risked choking.

Another round of teasing was directed at Michael's dumb comments regarding Jules's current state and he looked fed up. "At least I managed a decent proposal," he shot at Bobby whose grin didn't match the accusation.

Jedda watched as Piper tried unsuccessfully to make an inconspicuous slashing motion across her throat to stop the conversation.

"Do you see what my lovely fiancé is doing over there?" Bobby asked, still grinning widely. "She's begging you not to bring this up because, although none of you have noticed, there is no ring on her finger. She lost it."

"Misplaced it," Piper protested loudly. "It is somewhere in our house. I just can't find it at the moment." She looked sheepish and embarrassed, her cheeks pink.

"So I officially have a free pass on the proposal joke right now. No making fun of me about it until she finds her ring. She actually tried blaming Bruno. Like a dog could up and take her ring off the kitchen counter."

Jedda watched as laughter and camaraderie continued to pass between them all so fluidly. These were happy people, with an endless amount of joy.

When the dishes were cleared and the chatter was coming to a close Jedda thought he'd be saying goodbye to everyone. He assumed they'd all head out to their respective lives and he'd be left alone with his thoughts. An idea that made his nerves flare. He wasn't ready to be alone and maybe that was written clearly on his face, because they all kept making reasons to stay a bit longer.

Bobby lit the firepit by the porch and everyone settled in. It was eerily dark in all directions of the yard, the crackling fire and porch light only reaching out so far into the night, then the world dropped off into nothingness. It was quiet here, and it bordered on scary in Jedda's opinion.

He watched as Piper and Bobby settled onto the porch swing. Betty and Clay relaxed on two side-by-side rockers. Michael helped Jules slowly sink into the cushioned love seat and then sat beside her. There was one chair left, a kitchen chair that had clearly been added as an after thought. A spot squeezed in for the new guest.

"It's really peaceful out here," Jedda said, staring down into the crackling of the fire.

"I couldn't get used to it at first," Piper admitted as she rested her head on Bobby's shoulder. "It was almost creepy. I'd grown up in the city with so much noise, and being here, you have a lot of time to hear yourself think. That can be good and bad. Depends on what's going on in your head."

Jedda nodded his agreement. He was feeling the same way at the moment. He'd been fighting off the unnerving sensation for hours now. The inevitable moment when everyone would clear out, head home, and go to bed. Even Betty and Clay would eventually go upstairs and leave him alone for the night. He wasn't ready for things to be that quiet.

"So, Jedda, Michael mentioned to me that you used to cook in the prison kitchen. I'd love to chat with you some time about it," Clay said, rocking in unison with Betty.

"Sure, that'd be great. I like to help out. Do what I can."

Betty smiled at Jedda while patting Clay's hand. "You settle yourself in here first before we go putting you to work just yet."

The rumble of an approaching car and the cutting of headlights down the driveway drew everyone's attention.

"Anyone expecting company?" Michael asked as he stood to get a better look at the approaching car. Everyone paused for a minute then agreed they hadn't been the one to invite anyone over.

"It's Riley Dean Cook," Betty said, shaking her head and rolling her eyes. "Y'all do me a favor, let me handle this. R.D. and I go way back and I've got a good idea what he's coming here to say. I know y'all would like to jump in and give your two cents, but don't." Betty left no room for debate on the matter and Jedda watched as everyone fell obediently quiet. This is what people meant when they talked about Betty. This was the mysterious power she wielded. People listened to her, though Jedda hadn't figured out why yet.

"R.D.," Betty sang as the man in the police uniform approached the porch. "What brings you out here tonight? Liza and the kids are okay, I hope."

"Yes ma'am," R.D. said as he tipped the front of his police hat at the group on the porch. "They're doing fine and send their love."

"I heard about your promotion. Congratulations. Second in command on the force. Stan would be so proud of you."

"Thank you. That means a lot to me, Betty. With all the cleaning up they did after Judge Lions and Rylie, it opened up a lot of opportunities for guys like me who steered clear of the corruption."

"It's well-deserved," Betty said, widening her smile. "So are you here on business tonight, R.D.?"

"No, ma'am, this is a friendly visit. I want to give you a heads up about something that happened at the diner today. I assumed you'd heard already through the grapevine."

"The Edenville rumor mill does seem to be working overtime lately," Betty sighed.

"It's about your new house guest," R.D. said, intentionally not looking in Jedda's direction.

"He's right here. His name is Jedda."

"Good to meet you," Jedda said, though his heart was in his throat. Seeing a man in uniform, someone who could easily put him behind bars again, made him instantly uneasy.

"You as well," R.D. answered back with a quick glance in Jedda's direction before he went right back to talking about him like he wasn't there. "Betty, folks in town are worried about what you've got going on down here. They think you're bringing more danger here to Edenville. The people you've brought here in the past, they've caused lots of problems. The townsfolk don't want a repeat of that."

"I'm not sure I'm following you, R.D. I'd imagine you're talking about our sweet Piper here. I don't think she's ever done anything to hurt anyone in Edenville."

"Maybe not directly, but after she rolled into town we had a kidnapping—your own daughter no less, a serial killer on the loose, and, for hell's sake, a federal officer was gunned down on the stairs of St. Julian's church.

You can't really blame people for being worried when now you've got a convicted killer holed up here too."

"R.D.," Betty said with a furrowed brow of disappointment, "Piper didn't cause any of those things. She was a victim, and frankly she's lucky to be alive. Jedda has been paroled from prison. The court saw fit to let him go, and I don't see how anyone in town has any business making a fuss about it. So you can go on back there and tell them all to mind their own asses."

"Betty, I'm here as your friend."

"Oh, so you're saying today at the diner when this conversation came up you acted like a friend to me? You looked those ignorant folks in the eye and said, 'Any friend of Betty's is a friend of mine. If she believes this man deserves a second chance, then I trust her.' Or did you sit there and tell them not to worry, that you'd come up here and set me straight? That you'd give me a warning 'bout all this? Because if that's the approach you took, you and I need to talk about our definition of friendship. We're rowing different boats on that one."

"Bobby, could you please get my back on this? You're a cop, you understand the worry people must be having," R.D. said, pleading his case.

Bobby swallowed down a swig of his coffee and shook his head. "You've got to do better research before you come up here, R.D. Jedda is my brother. My folks adopted him before all that happened with his parents. If I've got anyone's back it's his and . . ." Betty shot a sideways glance at Bobby and he let his words trail off. Jedda took in again the quiet power of this woman, and he was starting to see where it came from.

"R.D., don't cast judgment on someone before you know him. I taught you that in Sunday school when you were a boy."

"You don't know him either, Betty. You don't know what prison has done to him or if he'll offend again. What gives you blind faith in the man?" He pointed over at Jedda who felt the heat blazing in his body. Not an angry fire, but a nervous one.

"You're acting like you're so different from him. We're all just one twist in the road away from where he is."

"That's a bit of a stretch, Betty. I read the police report. He killed two people in cold blood. His parents. You really want to say we're all on the verge of that?"

"You've lived here your whole life, R.D., which means you remember my daddy. He was a beast of a man. Hurt people just because of the color of their skin. Incited mobs of others to do the same."

"And you think he should have been killed?"

"He never laid a finger on me. I think if he'd directed any of that hate my way, or he ever looked at me with the intentions Jedda's father looked at Jedda's sister, I may have killed him. You know how quick my trigger finger is. But fate didn't twist it that way, so we'll never know. And what about you?"

"Are you suggesting I contemplated killing my parents? The preacher and the preacher's wife, really?"

"No. I'm not suggesting that. But I do vaguely remember you beating the hell out of Kyle Long for getting a little handsy with your sister after prom. Gave him a concussion didn't you? Sent him to the hospital."

"That's different," R.D. said, crossing his arms defensively and shaking his head.

"It is, but what if he'd gone too far? What if he'd taken from your sister something she could never get back? Her innocence. Would you have stopped at a concussion? If one thing in our lives woulda been different we could be walking in his shoes, and you know what that tells me? We're only a few steps away from being where he is, and more important than that, it means he's only a few steps away from finding his way back to where we are. I think it's our job to help him do so."

R.D. was silent as he hung his head and gritted his teeth at the truth being spat in his direction. Jedda could see the tension in his jaw even from the distance between them. "One of these days, Betty, all these stray dogs you keep taking in, you're going to get bitten."

"Well that'll learn me won't it, R.D. But you know, I'd rather find out I was wrong the hard way than start wrong and stay wrong. You're in here talking like I have a decision to make. Like putting this boy out on the street is some kind of choice for me. You're the one who has a choice here."

"And what's that?"

"Next time folks are talking 'bout him, talking 'bout me, you need to decide what kind of man you're going be. The kind that stands up for someone who's trying to start his life over and not doing anyone no harm, or if you'll stand with the people trying to knock him down before he's even gotten himself up yet."

"You know how things are here. I'm worried folks are gonna try to run him out of town. Try to put him in a position that gets him tossed back in jail. For good."

"Don't let them."

"It ain't that simple."

"It's as simple as you make it. I know you have a good heart, R.D. Your mama taught you how to give people a chance. So try it."

R.D. dropped his head like a soldier waving his white flag in defeat. "I'll give your love to the girls," he said, backing down the steps of the porch. "Just try to stay out of trouble."

"He will," Betty promised.

"I was talking to you," R.D. said, causing a small chuckle to roll across the porch.

"Night, R.D.," Betty called, starting to rock her chair nonchalantly again, as though nothing had happened.

"Jedda," she started as she sipped at her hot coffee, "I'm sorry you had to see such ignorance up close and personal."

"I guess I underestimated the intolerance here in Edenville," Michael groaned, shaking his head at R.D.'s brake lights pulling away.

"I should be the one apologizing. I wasn't looking to bring you guys any trouble here."

Jules snickered a bit and looked over at Piper. "Well unless you have a time machine that can take us back before we met this one," she raised her thumb and gestured over to the porch swing, "then it's a little too late for that. If you're bringing trouble here, you're in good company."

"Hey," Piper shot back defensively, "I tried to get you guys to leave me alone. You're all just so damn persistent.

"Oh cut the crap," Bobby said, looking down into Piper's serious face. "You loved it. You couldn't stay away."

"There are days I'm still trying to get out of here," Michael teased, immediately bracing himself for Jules's slap against his arm, which came just as he expected. "But seriously, Jedda, just lay low. You are on a no-strike program. Any type of infraction will land you back in jail. For good. Just stay here, and relax."

When the conversation turned back to something else and the laughter was rolling once more throughout the group, Jules leaned over to Jedda as if she had something to say.

"I won't let this town turn you into a prisoner in this house. Tomorrow you and I are breaking out of here." The smile that spread across her lips was one of pure mischief and made a knot form in Jedda's already nervous stomach.

"But Michael said—" Jedda began, but Jules's dismissive hand waved off his words.

"The man called me fat, how smart could he be? Just trust me, tomorrow I'll get you out of here."

Jedda smiled and nodded as he leaned back into his chair, away from the hush-hush conversation with Jules. Maybe the cliché about redheads was true. Maybe they were trouble. He guessed by this time tomorrow he'd be finding out.

Chapter Three

Willow couldn't pinpoint exactly what was making her feel like she was about to lose her lunch. Maybe it was the bouncing of the bus on the barely paved roads of this impossibly small town. Or the fumes from the exhaust that were mixing with the cologne of the man who'd sat down next to her, rather than taking one of the many other empty seats. More likely though, it was what had gotten her on this bus in the first place that was turning her stomach. Bad choices and old habits were probably to blame for the burning and swirling she felt inside.

Up until this point, she'd done so well for so long. She'd been above all of the things she'd escaped. But now that her past was nipping at her heels again it felt like the world was falling in on her. She jumped as the overhead intercom rang out. "Next stop, Main Street, Edenville," the driver announced as the brakes began to squeal to a stop.

Michael had told Willow to wait. He'd instructed her that he would contact her over her school's spring break if he felt Jedda was ready to see her. A plane ticket would be arranged and her parents could join her for extra support if she wanted. But Willow couldn't wait that long. She wasn't sure she'd even survive until spring break if she stayed in New York. Going back home to Block Island wasn't an option either. Her only hope was to slip away to this tiny southern town and buy some time. To count on her brother for protection, just as she had all those years ago.

She squeezed her way by the man sitting next to her and grabbed her bag as she hopped off the bus. Fishing out her phone, she pulled up Michael's number. Surely he wouldn't turn her away if she were already here. He wouldn't leave her here on Main Street just because she'd ignored his suggestions. Or so she hoped.

As she walked down the sunny side of Main Street looking for a quiet place to make her call, a commotion caught her eye. Did they have commotions here in Edenville? What could they possibly argue about? Cows? Grass? Fences? Because judging the scenery for the last half hour on the bus, that's all they seemed to have. Her curiosity brought her closer to the circle of people gathered in front of the general store. She stood behind a tall man in a painter's jumpsuit and peeked her head around his shoulder.

A small but very pregnant redhead was standing with her hands perched on her hips, her skin flushed nearly as bright as her hair. Next to her was . . . Willow took in a quick breath as she realized who the man standing next to this very angry woman was. It was her brother. Jedda looked entirely different from the day he'd freed her from the chains that kept her tied to the radiator in their parents' house. His arms and shoulders had doubled in size, his hair was longer and slicked back, but was the same shade of shadowy black it had always been. He was taller, wider, and now had beard stubble on his cheeks and chin. But his eyes were exactly the same. Green, piercing, and almond shaped. The slant of his nose and the curve of his chin made it perfectly clear to her that this was her brother. Once that sunk in, all she could ask herself was, why was he in the center of a circle of people who looked like a lynch mob ready to strike? She leaned in to listen as the redhead began to speak.

"Everything I need for my wedding reception is in there, and you're telling me you won't let me in?" she shouted, her voice fierce and demanding.

"Here at Clint's General Store we have the right to refuse to serve anyone we see fit. Isn't that right, Toby?" the man blocking the store entrance asked the police officer who'd just walked up.

"He's right, Jules. It's his store and he can turn you away if he wants to," the officer said, moving next to the owner of the store.

"This is horse shit, Toby. I've put a hefty down payment on all that equipment," the redhead shot back, her finger pointing accusingly at them.

Jedda was standing stone-faced, sweat beading across his forehead and Willow worried what these people might want—what they might do.

"And we'll be happy to refund you," the storeowner said smugly.

"Shut the hell up, Clint. You're acting like a damn fool. I don't want my money back. I want the equipment I need for my wedding."

"Then maybe you should have thought about that before you came down here with mixed company." The store owner gestured at Jedda as though he were a stray dog. "Everyone knows your ma is a coot, but I didn't think you'd be dumb enough to mess around with a killer. Don't that man of yours give a damn what kind of men you run around with? Or is this your new man?" Clint spat a mouthful of chewing tobacco to the ground, splattering Jules's white sneaker.

"You listen here," she said, taking five large steps forward and cutting the distance between her very pregnant belly and the man blocking the door to a few inches. “You want to call me a floosy, you want to insult the company I keep? Fine. But you know better than to call my ma any kind of name out here on Main Street. People won’t stand for that. I won’t have it. She’s done more for this town than anyone else I know. Someone doesn’t have enough money for food, who’s bringing them over groceries? A death in the family, my ma is the first one there with a casserole. This store was about to go under two years ago and Ma got everyone in town together and got them to stop driving the thirty miles to the big-box stores and bring their business back to you. So the next words out of your mouth better be, ‘You tell your ma, I’m sorry’ or you and I are going to have a problem, Clint.”

Willow felt her heart thudding hard against the walls of her chest. Who was this pregnant nut job and what was she about to do? How did they settle things down in a town like Edenville? A showdown?

“Take that murderer and get out of here,” Clint hissed, leaning down into Jules’s face.

Seeming completely shocked by his rebuttal, Jules looked as though she planned to turn around and walk away. Apparently though, the twist in her hips was just a means of leverage as she slammed her knee into the store owner’s crotch. The wind that escaped his lungs was an audible huff of pain and he dropped down hard to his knees. The man was whimpering and trying desperately to speak. “Toby, a-a-a-rrest that bitch,” he managed to whisper.

Toby, looking as shocked as the crowd that had gathered, put his hand behind his back to reach for his handcuffs.

"Toby Ray Dunderson, if you even think about putting handcuffs on me or arresting me when I am this pregnant I will have my mother call your mother so fast you won't know what hit you. You really want to see what your mama does to you when she finds out you put me in early labor? Now Clint here seems to have been taken by some kind of fit. You might want to get him some help," Jules said as she spun on her heels and grabbed pale-faced Jedda's arm to quickly follow her. As they blew past, Willow ducked her face, though she wasn't sure why. As they strode away from her at a fast pace, she remembered there was no reason to hide from them. She was going where they were going. Hopefully.

"Jedda," she called out as she jogged to catch up with them. They both spun to look at her but only Jedda stopped in his tracks, leaving Jules to tug at his arm.

"We need to get on back to the house," Jules insisted, pulling at him again.

"I-I-I can't breathe," Jedda stuttered, putting his hand up to his heart. "My chest. It's killing me." The blood drained from his face and Willow's jog turned to a run.

"Are you okay?" she asked, letting Jedda brace himself on her.

"Who are you?" Jules asked defensively standing between Willow and Jedda.

"I'm his sister." Willow looked up into her brother's face, hoping he'd recognize her.

"Willow?" Jules asked, eying her skeptically. "Well then get in the car. We need to get out of here."

Jedda's breath was rapid and broken as he flopped into the passenger seat of Jules's car. Willow climbed in the back behind him.

"What's the matter, Jedda?" Jules asked as she backed up and raced the car down the street.

"I don't know. This pain. My chest. I'm dizzy and I can't breathe. Something isn't . . ." The words escaped him as he rested his head against the glass of the car window.

"We need to get him to a hospital," Willow shouted as she leaned forward and put her hand on his shoulder. "Something's wrong." The thought of reuniting with her brother just to watch him die was a cruel joke she was sure the universe was plenty capable of.

"I don't think it's a good idea. They'll know who he is. Word's gotten all over town by now. I wouldn't trust anyone. But I do know a doctor who I trust with my life. I'll take you to him." Jules turned the car around quickly and sped back past the crowd of people who still hovered over a hunched Clint.

Willow stayed silent for the five-minute drive that was filled with her brother's labored breathing and sweat pouring down his temples.

"We're here. Can you walk?" Jules asked as she hopped out of the car and waited for his reply. Willow marveled at Jules's nimbleness given the size of her protruding belly. The woman could fight and run.

"Yes," he mustered between short breaths and pushed his car door open. Willow was at his side in a flash, supporting as much of his weight as she could. He towered a foot over her, but she was trying her best. Jules raced in the door ahead of them as Willow read the sign.

"Wait!" she shouted grabbing Jules's attention. "You can't be serious. This is a gynecologist." She halted Jedda from walking any farther.

"He's my friend and my obstetrician. He can help. I trust him, now hurry up." Jules held open the door and waved them in.

"Josh! Josh, are you here?" Jules called as she blew right passed the receptionist desk and motioned for Willow and Jedda to do the same.

"Jules?" A handsome young man in a doctor's coat came flying out of his office. "Are you in labor? Contractions?"

"No. I need help. This here is my friend Jedda and there is something wrong with him. I think he's having a heart attack."

The man shifted his stare from Jules to Jedda and then back again. "Is he pregnant?" he asked, shaking his head in disbelief.

"No. Don't be an idiot, Josh. You see, people haven't taken very kindly to him being here and I was afraid to take him to the hospital."

"I know who he is," Josh answered quietly. "But I can't help him unless he has ovaries."

"Shut the hell up, Josh. I've known you my whole life. Our fathers were best friends. I know you spent ages working in the ER before you picked your specialty. You can help him. So help him," Jules demanded as she planted her hands on her hips.

Indignation spread across the doctor's face; he looked ready to argue, but suddenly that washed away as he took another look at Jedda. "Bring him in here. I'll do what I can, but if his life is in danger I'm calling an ambulance."

Jedda plopped himself down on the examination table and Josh instructed him to lie back. "I'm sure these won't be necessary," he said as he collapsed the stirrups and examination light.

"Do you have any allergies that you know of? Were you eating or drinking any new or unusual things prior to the onset of symptoms?"

Jedda shook his head no as he gasped for more breath.

"A family history or personal history of heart problems, murmurs, valve issues?"

Again Jedda shook his head no.

"Tell me exactly what you're feeling."

"I can't breathe and my chest is killing me. Like a knife is in it. Everything is spinning," Jedda mustered as he leaned back on the paper-covered table.

"What happened right before the symptoms started?" Josh asked as he pressed his finger to Jedda's wrist and stared down at his watch.

When Jedda couldn't form the words, Willow chimed in. "She was kicking some guy in the junk." Her finger pointed accusingly at Jules.

"You assaulted someone?" Josh asked, slipping a thermometer under Jedda's tongue.

"No, it was Clint Masterson. That's more like animal abuse than assault. He was asking for it. He was calling Ma names and a big group had gathered in around us. They were giving Jedda a hard time and I may have overreacted."

"Jedda, do you have any history of panic or anxiety attacks?" Josh asked as he set his stethoscope on Jedda's chest and asked him to try to take a deep breath. "I can't give you any medication, Jedda, as you aren't my patient and I could get in a lot of trouble for it, but I think you might be experiencing a panic attack." Slipping a blood pressure cuff on Jedda's arm, Josh continued, "Your heart rate is high, you're sweating, and," he watched the beeping monitor in front of him, "your blood pressure is high as well. But if you're not experiencing any other symptoms and have no history of heart or health problems, then my gut tells me that's what's happening."

"Your gut tells you?" Willow asked incredulously with a look of skepticism.

"If you'd like a more scientific answer then I'd suggest you call an ambulance and have him admitted to the hospital."

"No," Jules said, touching Willow's shoulder gently. "Jedda doesn't need any reason to be locked back up, and I would be afraid what would happen if a doctor could call him crazy down here. What can you do for him, Josh?"

"Nothing." Josh wrapped his stethoscope back around his neck. "Well, not much. Jedda you've got to get yourself through this. You need to close your eyes and imagine a place where you feel safe, happy, and comfortable. I'm going to go grab a paper bag for you to breathe into. I know it sounds silly, but it can help." Josh walked quickly out of the room and down the hall to look for a bag.

"Are you thinking of a place, Jedda?" Willow asked as she sidled up to her brother.

"Yes," he answered, his eyes clenched closed. "I'm in my cell. It's quiet and I'm sitting on my bed, reading a book."

Willow and Jules locked eyes and a sad realization fell over their faces. Prison felt safer to Jedda than anywhere else in the world. That was his happiest place.

"Okay, here's the bag," Josh said as he made his way back to Jedda's side. He pulled his phone from his pocket and began studying the screen. "I'm going to play you some music. Is there a song that makes you feel particularly calm?"

Jedda shrugged as he breathed into the bag rhythmically. Willow cleared her throat and took another step closer to her brother. She tried to block out the wide eyes of Jules and Josh as lyrics began to escape her mouth. "Climbing up the highest hill . . ." Her voice was a raspy emotion-filled tremble but its beauty seemed to fill the room. "To the top to get a thrill." Jedda's eyes were open now, and he stared at his sister with a gratitude that couldn't be measured in words. "I'll be right there to catch you if you start to fall." Her voice grew stronger and louder and with it Jedda seemed to calm.

"Keep going," Josh urged, checking Jedda's pulse again.

"We'll always be together, I'll be there when you call. You have me as your best friend forever, there's no doubt. No matter what the trouble, we'll always make it out."

"Your voice is absolutely beautiful," Jules said, mindlessly stroking her belly, making sure her baby heard the lullaby. "What song is that?"

"Jedda used to sing it to me when . . . he just used to sing it to me when I needed to hear it." Willow discreetly wiped away a tear and touched her brother's arm. "Are you feeling better?"

"Starting to," he said into the bag.

Josh looked down at his vibrating pager. "You need to stay here for a bit and relax. Then, if your symptoms subside completely, I'll let you go. You should see a professional though. These attacks won't always be so easily subdued and you won't know when they will strike. They can be truly dangerous to your health in the wrong circumstances."

"Thank you, Josh." Jules smiled at the man gratefully.

"And you," he said, pointing a finger in her face. "You are pregnant. Very pregnant and you cannot go around picking fights, being physical, and stressing yourself out. You've got more to worry about than just yourself now and you need to be more careful. I swear you're the same little girl who I used to have to pull off the other kids on the playground. My dad told me to keep an eye on you when you started school, but I don't think he understood how big of a job that was. Do I need to call Michael?"

"No." Jules hung her head and rolled her eyes like a scolded teenager. "I promise I'll stop kicking guys even if they deserve it. At least until the baby is born."

"Sure you will." Josh patted Jedda on the shoulder in a gesture of farewell and stepped out of the room.

"Do you kick a lot of guys in the nuts?" Willow asked as she sat in the chair next to Jedda.

"Let's just say it's been harder for me to give up than alcohol was. It's not my fault. Every now and then guys just need it. It's like a reset button for their brains."

With that Jedda let out a chuckle and brought himself to a sitting position, taking the bag away from his face. "Do me a favor, if I ever get close to needing a reset, give me a little warning."

"Am I that bad?" Jules asked, lighting up with a flattered smile.

"I spent years in jail and even I think you're a bad ass."

"Oh stop, really?" she asked, blushing and shooing him off with a smile and a brush of her hand.

"Um, I don't think he meant that as a compliment," Willow said as she twisted her face up at Jules.

"Sweetie, you're either a doormat or a badass. You'll never see any boots treading on me."

Chapter Four

"Just so we're clear," Michael's voice boomed across Betty's kitchen, "no one is ever going to listen to me, right? I know I told you not to make a big deal the night Jedda arrived," he said, pointing at Betty, who was uncharacteristically meek this evening. "And I told you to wait until Jedda had more time to adjust before you came down to see him," Michael continued, changing his attention to Willow whose eyes were darting around the room. "And you, Jules, you are killing me. You of all people should listen to me. We're about to be married, have a baby. You go out assaulting people, parading Jedda down Main Street even though I told you not to. You should know better." Michael ran his hand through his hair in exasperation, shaking his head in disappointment.

"Well, Your Honor, in my defense," Jules began, looking coyly over at her fiancé, "historically I've never really known better, or done what anyone has told me to do. So really it's you who should have known better about me knowing better. If I were you I wouldn't have taken your eyes off me for a second. My track record speaks for itself. I can't be trusted. So this is kind of on you."

"And as far as anyone heeding your advice, boy," Betty joined in, "you're about to marry my daughter who is about to give birth to my granddaughter. That's a long line of people who will probably never listen to what you say. I'm afraid this is just the beginning."

Jedda's eyes moved from face to face in the room, unable to decipher what was a joke and who found it funny. Glancing at his sister he realized she, too, was wondering the same thing.

"You are all a giant pain in my ass. You got pretty damn lucky today that you didn't get arrested and that Jedda was able to bounce back from whatever got him all spun around there. Did you really take him to your gynecologist?" Michael asked, twisting his face, looking half amused and half shocked.

"The Pap smear was a bit of a shock, but otherwise, he was very helpful," Jedda said, taking a leap in the direction of humor. Maybe it was too soon, maybe it would result in more scolding, but there was a chance it could break this moment and he wanted to be a part of that. Within a second he had his answer. Betty howled a loud laugh as she slapped her knee and Jules broke into a giddy fit that had her doubled over her big belly. Even Michael and Willow were stifling their laughter.

"You got lucky today," Michael repeated, trying to stiffen his lips to fend off a smile. "No more taking chances like that. Are you sure you're feeling better?"

"Josh recommended I get back into a routine. I'm going to start my workout again tomorrow. That was a big part of my day and always helped me feel focused. I'll have to improvise for workout equipment but I know it will help."

As everyone nodded in agreement, the screen door squeaked open and Bobby and Piper stepped into the kitchen, both looking solemn.

"Hey," Bobby said, forcing a smile. He scanned the room and fought shock as he addressed Willow. "You are here? I mean you're here already. Good to see you again." He crossed the room and she stood to hug them both.

Bobby jammed his hands into his pocket and turned his attention to Michael and Jedda. "Can I talk to you two outside for a minute?" The question seemed to carry with it the obvious note of trouble and tension.

Michael rolled his eyes, "I already know about what Jules did today. Are they pressing charges, is that what this is about?"

"No, they're too scared of Betty and their own mothers to do anything. But speaking of that—Jules, cut the crap. You're going to put yourself into labor. Now guys, come on outside so I can talk to you two," Bobby repeated, pointing at Jedda and Michael.

Jedda felt a rock sitting in his stomach as he stepped onto the porch. Every step felt closer to bad news: one moment away from being told he was heading back to prison. He didn't know what was more frightening to him, the fact that prison felt more like home than anywhere else he'd ever been, or that he could be sent back and never be let out. Both ideas were suffocating.

"When did Willow show up?" Bobby asked in a hushed voice as he leaned himself against the porch railing and crossed his boots over each other.

"She was downtown just in time to see the show Jules was putting on. I guess she took the bus. Why?" Michael asked, and Jedda took note of the fact that he seemed to know his friend well enough to read that something was the matter.

"I got a call today. It was from a detective up in New York. He was looking for her. He said something about the assault charges being dropped. Honestly it felt more like a threat than a call of concern. He was trying to find her."

"Did you tell him she was here?" Jedda asked, feeling heat roll across his body.

"No. I didn't even know she was here, but I could tell from the start something wasn't right. I wouldn't have said anything even if I had known she was in Edenville. Has she told you why she's here early? Anything about some trouble she might be in?"

"She hasn't said anything," Michael chimed in, folding his arms across his chest. "Like barely a word. Is she normally so quiet?"

Bobby shrugged his shoulders, "I have no clue. I've only met her once and talked to her on the phone a few times about Jedda. She looks different than the last time I saw her. She dropped some of the edgy stuff she was wearing last time. She seems much more casual, less the tortured artist this time. Other than that, I don't really have a baseline. Last I heard, school was great. She was making friends, loving it."

"Did someone assault her or she assaulted someone?" Jedda asked, pacing around the porch and feeling his heart starting to race again.

"Jedda, take a seat. You can't get yourself worked up. Whatever it is, she's safe now. We're not going to let anything happen to her," Michael assured him.

"Well I dug around and everything has been retracted. Someone had the report wiped out, and that's what the call was about. Wanting me to let Willow know that the charges were not being pursued. I couldn't find out who else was involved. I'm going to call in some favors, and see what I can uncover."

"No," Michael said, heading back for the screen door. "This is ridiculous. The only person here that's at a real risk of anything is Jedda and no one seems to realize how dangerous any kind of trouble can be for him. The girl is a grown-up, she can fess up to whatever the hell is going on."

He stormed back into the house, Jedda and Bobby following closely behind, but neither said anything.

"Willow." Michael's voice was rough again and the conversation that was filled with the buzzing of excited women cut off quickly. "The assault charges in New York, what happened? What are they about, and why were they dropped?"

"They were dropped?" Willow asked, her eyes wide. She shook her head to center herself back in the moment. "I mean, how do you know about that?"

"Because Bobby got a call from a detective up there today asking if you were here."

"Shit." Willow stood quickly, sliding into her coat and trying to make her way closer to the door, before multiple people blocked her way.

"Where are you going?" Michael asked, gesturing that she sit back down.

"If they're calling that means he already knows where I am. I'm sorry, Jedda, but I've got to go. I'll call you soon," she promised as she tried again to get back toward the door.

"Sit down," Michael said in an oddly paternal voice that he apparently had grown into overnight now that he was on the cusp of being a father.

Willow stopped in her tracks but didn't make a move to sit back down. Jedda's heart was thumping hard again as he tried to piece together what was happening.

"Excuse me?" Willow asked, raising an eyebrow in indignation. "Who the hell do you think you are? I'm free to come and go as I damn well please." This was a side of Willow Jedda hadn't prepared for. He still had the image of her meek body and small voice burned into his mind. A grown-up Willow with loads of attitude was quickly shattering that memory.

The stunned silence of the room was broken by Betty's cool voice. "She's right, Michael. She's a grown woman. You let her go. Do you plan to walk, sweetie?"

"Yes," Willow said, shrugging her shoulders. "I can find my way back to the bus stop."

"I don't doubt that you can. It's about an hour and half walk. The sun is setting now, too."

"I run cross country. I'll be fine."

"You might run cross country, but you ain't never run cross this country, so let me get you a couple of things." Betty moved to a drawer in her kitchen. "Here, take this whistle. It's not a foolproof way to keep the bears away but it's better than nothing if you come across one. Blow the dickens out of it and you might be okay. The whistle won't work for the coyote though, them being dogs and all, they seem to like the sound of it. You'll need something like this," Betty said, handing her a pot and wooden spoon. "If you whack this hard enough you should scare it off. Now, if there is a pack of them, they tend to be bolder, so don't hold it against me if one flanks you while another chases you and the pot doesn't do enough to keep them at bay." Willow took the pan and spoon but it seemed to be more out of shock than an acceptance of the fact that she'd need them. "Here is a flashlight. The road back has quite a few drops off the side. If you find yourself running from the wildlife the worst thing that can happen to you is taking a tumble into a ravine. It could be days before someone finds you." Betty tucked the flashlight under Willow's full arms. "Now do you have any pepper spray or anything? The only thing more dangerous than the bears is some of the highland folk here who don't come down the mountain too often. They see a pretty girl like you walking alone, I don't want to think what they could do."

"I know what you're doing," Willow said, rolling her eyes and huffing. "You're not going to scare me out of leaving. There are things scarier in the world than what you just listed."

"Willow," Piper said, stepping forward. "What's scaring you? If you're in some kind of trouble, we can help you. You're safe here, but you need to tell us what's going on."

"Actually, I don't. I don't even know any of you. I'm happy for what you're doing for Jedda, but I can assure you that I don't need the same thing. I've got a completely different life than him. My parents, they're doctors. We live in, like, a giant house, and I have everything I need already. I'm different than him. So help him and let me go."

"Please," Jedda pleaded as he stood between Willow and the front door. "Just stay tonight and if you still want to go in the morning then I'm sure someone will drive you back to the bus."

Betty extended her hands to take back all the supplies she'd given to Willow. Reluctantly the girl dropped them back into her arms. "I'll stay tonight, but I'm leaving in the morning."

After a moment of nervous silence in the room, Betty spoke up. "Who's hungry? I've got a roast to put in the oven. Everything looks better on a full belly. Maybe you'll feel like chatting once you've eaten."

"I'm a vegetarian," Willow said with an air of superiority.

"Oh, well then, the bears probably would have left you alone. They like their snacks with more flavor."

* * * *

Jedda knew he should be sleeping. That's what people did at three o'clock in the morning but all he could think about was his sister being assaulted. He thought of what might have happened to her, and the only thing that bothered him more than that image was the free-fall of crazed, uncontrollable anger he felt seething inside of him. He paced the small living room where he was supposed to be sleeping, but each lap he took made him feel more like a caged animal. He needed air. He needed space.

He slammed the palms of his hands against his sweat-covered forehead, willing his mind to stop spinning. He felt like his senses were completely overloaded. He'd gone from having so little to deal with to suddenly having far too much. Grabbing his sweatshirt, he headed as quietly as possible for the front door. Flashing for a minute to Betty's warnings about bears and coyotes, he grabbed a flashlight and the whistle, just in case there was any truth in her words.

He went down the front porch steps and stood out in front of the house staring up at the sky. So many people took the sky for granted. They could go outside and stare up at it any time they wanted. He stepped out farther and farther from the house, never looking down, staring straight up to the bright and pitted surface of the moon.

When he heard a rustling to his left, he immediately clutched the whistle tight in his hand. He was a fast runner, prison had given him plenty of time to become incredibly fit, but he was no match for a bear as far as he knew. As he shifted on his feet, ready to head back to the house, he heard a voice.

"I could shoot you right now and be well within the law," a man said as he stepped forward out of the shadows, a gun dangling in his hands.

"I don't want any trouble," Jedda assured him as he raised his hands, showing they only held a whistle.

"My house is just over that hill and down the road a ways. I was out walking my dog and came across this crazy man wandering around. He attacked me and I shot him," the man said with a whistling speech impediment. "Once they realize you was that killer, they'd know I was telling the truth."

"I was just out for a walk myself," Jedda said as he took two tentative steps back. "I'm heading back to the house now."

"Ain't nobody wanting you here. We don't need no more trouble in this town than Betty's already brought us. You ain't welcome."

Jedda hadn't fully recovered from the rage he'd been feeling in the house at the thought of Willow being hurt again. His muscles were still tense and jumping from the urge to dismember whoever it was that had his sister so scared. He could tell even now, as the man with the gun glared at him under the moonlight, that given the chance he could easily lose control and find himself back in jail. While he should have been afraid of the man with the gun, he felt only fear for his own capabilities, his own reactions.

"Rumor has it you got a sister here with you. Can't imagine what she's into. Likely as much of a degenerate as you. She ain't welcome here either, and I'll be happy to give her that message when I see her too." The man smiled, showing his yellowed and missing teeth, as though he'd just won a battle.

Jedda had been standing on the edge of out of control and those words had just shoved him over. "You want to see me attack you?" he growled as he lowered his hands and changed his stance from a running one, to a fighting one. "You don't threaten my sister. Gun or not, I'll make you regret it." The man's face blurred in front of Jedda's eyes. He flashed back to many years before, to the marks Willow had the day he found her at their parents' apartment. He didn't care if this man shot him, because in his mind he wasn't even here, he was miles away, years ago, and he was full to the brim with blind hatred.

The flash of another light drew his eye out to the woods behind the man with the gun and out stepped R.D., one hand on his hip just above his weapon, the other shining a flashlight they way only cops do. "Darren, don't make me shoot you. It's late and I don't feel like doing the paperwork."

"R.D., this man is threatening my life. You see that look in his eye, he's crazy."

"Well he's crazy on the property where he's a guest. While you, on the other hand, must have taken a wrong turn somewhere."

"I was walking my dog," Darren hissed as he tightened his grip on his gun.

"I don't see a dog," R. D. said as he walked up and stood next to Jedda. "I do however see your gun. Put that damn thing away and get on out of here. This ain't the Wild West, and you sure as hell ain't no cowboy."

"He's a killer. You want him just roaming around this close to your land at three o'clock in the morning?"

"At this point I'm more worried about the fact that I've got your stupid ass as a neighbor. Jedda hasn't done anything wrong that I can see. Any friend of Betty's is a friend of mine," he said, knowingly parroting back Betty's words from earlier that day. "If I see him break the law, I'll be the first one to put him away. Until then, you and all your buddies will leave him alone. You hear?"

Darren grunted his acknowledgement and turned on his heels to head back toward his own property.

"You shouldn't be out here wandering around this late," R.D. said as he folded his arms over his chest and watched Darren disappear into the woods.

"I needed some air. Adjusting to being out is harder than I thought. I figured if I could get out here maybe it would make some sense."

"I find that whether you're coming out of prison or not, life don't make too much sense. The more time you spend trying to figure it out, the more you start feeling like you're losing control. I heard what happened down in town today, and Bobby briefed me on what's going on with your little sister. I don't know what you plan to do with all that, but I can tell you one thing, these folks are all standing around waiting for you to screw up so they can kill you or have you tossed in jail . . . and they'd rather kill you if they had their choice."

"I almost lost it on that guy," Jedda admitted as he kicked at a stone.

"I know, I was watching. I wasn't going to let him shoot you but honestly I was more interested in how you were going to react. I know Darren; he's a moron and a coward. He doesn't have the stomach to follow through on his threats. But I could see you on the other hand look perfectly capable."

"I should go back in," Jedda said, rubbing at his burning tired eyes. "Thanks for . . . well thanks."

"I live across the way there," R.D. said, pointing up over the ridge. "I was just finishing up my shift, on my way home, and saw that moron leave his house with a gun. I thought there was a chance he was heading your way. But I'm not always going to be around to jump in. You need to figure out if you can stop yourself. They aren't going to stop hounding you. Can you walk away?"

"Hopefully." Jedda swallowed hard as he thought of what he had almost done to Darren, and the fact that R.D. would have been watching. He was a split second away from finding himself back behind bars, back away from Willow again. Leaving her out here with whatever problem she was facing. "I can," he said, nodding his head again. "I have to."

As Jedda stepped back into the house he was shocked to see Clay standing in the kitchen making a cup of tea.

"Sorry, did I wake you?" Jedda asked, slipping out of his sweatshirt.

"No you didn't wake me." He offered a cup to Jedda. "That idiot Darren woke me up. I heard him running his mouth. He's always causing trouble around here for one reason or another. He came down and gave me hell about how I was smelling up his yard with my fancy food."

"Fancy food?" Jedda asked wondering what kind of meal could be enough to be considered a nuisance by the neighbors.

"I was making a corn beef roast out in my smoker. He was acting like I was cooking skunks or something."

"Smoked corned beef? I've never had that before. The one they serve in prison on Saint Patrick's day is like shoe leather with soggy cabbage. I always wanted to try it with this recipe I saw. Roasted brussels sprout in balsamic vinaigrette. That's how I used to pass the time most days. Dreaming up and reading about ways to fix the food in there. It bordered on inedible.

"He's just lucky Betty sleeps like a corpse. She would have taken his knees out with her shotgun if she'd seen him giving you a hard time. She can't stand the man."

Jedda took the mug of tea and breathed in the hot earthy steam. "I'm worried about Willow leaving tomorrow."

"She's not going anywhere," Clay said, pulling out a kitchen chair and gesturing for Jedda to join him.

"What do you mean? She's dead set on going."

"Betty doesn't want her to go, and Betty always get's what she wants. One way or another she'll figure out a way to get her to stay, and more than that, she'll probably make her think it was her own idea all along."

"How did Betty get so incredibly . . ." Jedda hesitated, not knowing the right word.

"Stop right there," Clay said, halting Jedda's attempt with his hand. "There is no adjective. No word. You'll wrack your brain all night and never come up with one. I'm not sure how she got the way she is, but it's fun as hell to sit back and watch it. She marched into the kitchen of my very upscale New York restaurant and asked me to jot down my recipes. That's how we met. In that very moment I knew I loved her, and we've spent nearly every minute together since. I gave up everything I had up in the city, all my tenure in that position as a head chef to come down to this little town and open a restaurant that most people will probably not even understand down here, but do you know why I did that?"

Jedda shrugged, "Why?"

“I have no goddamn idea. That’s the point. She wanted me down here and somehow in the face of all better logic, here I am. I don’t know exactly how she did it, I just know when that woman has her mind or heart set on something, it’s a forgone conclusion. So your sister isn’t leaving tomorrow,” Clay said, shrugging his shoulders. “Now do you think you can sleep?”

Jedda put his tea down on the table and rubbed his eyes. “Actually, yes,” he smirked as he stood and headed back to the living room.

“And Jedda, one more thing,” Clay called over his shoulder. “Even though I’m not sure how I ended up here, I’ve never been happier. That’s the point. She doesn’t do these things lightly, or for her own pleasure. When she moves a chess piece on the board, it isn’t so she can win; it’s to move the game forward. She’s just keeping us all moving forward.”

Chapter Five

"I really do appreciate the hospitality last night, Betty," Willow said as she stuffed her clothes back into her bag. Jedda nodded his approval at his sister's attitude adjustment. "Do you know when Michael will be back to take me to the bus station?"

"He said in a couple hours. He had a meeting he couldn't skip," Betty answered, trying to busy herself with the dishes.

"Now, Willow, I hear you're a singer. Would you be so kind as to give us a little song this morning?" Betty asked, pulling up a chair next to her.

"I don't really sing much lately. It's something I have to feel, you know what I mean? And I don't feel it right now. Sorry."

"That's no problem. I know what you mean," Betty said, patting her hand lightly. "My husband used to play guitar and sing around the fire."

"Clay?" Willow asked, fiddling with the zipper on her bag.

"No, Clay and I aren't married. I'm livin' in sin. Something I thought I'd never do, but you get to a certain age and you just can't see the point in a big wedding and putting that pressure on yourself. If it ain't broke don't fix it, and there ain't nothing broke between Clay and me."

Willow nodded her head as though she understood, but made a face as though that was far too much information.

"Oh well, that didn't really answer your question did it?" Betty asked, slapping her hand to her forehead. "My husband's name was Stan. He was a police officer. He was killed in the line of duty twelve years ago. That's Jules's father. He was a wonderful man."

"I'm sorry to hear that," Willow said, finding a million places to look except toward Betty.

"It's all part of the plan I suppose. God never gives us more than we can handle. I know I'm right where I'm meant to be. Sitting here with you two. Is that how you feel, Willow, that you're right where you're meant to be?" Betty's laser beam eyes connected with Willow's.

"I know what you're doing." Willow laughed. "You are very good, I bet you get most people to open right up to you, don't you?"

"Usually," Betty said, raising an eyebrow. "You'll come around. They all do." She poured a little more juice into Willow's glass.

A quiet knock on the door sent Betty's back straight as she looked out to try to see who it might be.

"Is Michael back?" Willow asked, reaching anxiously for her bag.

"He don't knock. Nobody who's welcomed here knocks, really." She pushed her chair back and headed for the door. Willow jumped to her feet and followed. Maybe whoever it was would give her a damn ride to the bus stop.

When she rounded the corner she felt the air escape her lungs and the blood drain from her face. Right there, standing on the other side of the screen door, was Brad. His green pinstriped oxford shirt was tucked perfectly into his pressed pleated khakis. His hair was tamed with gel and his smile at the sight of Betty approaching was convincingly innocent.

"You selling Bibles, boy?" Betty asked through the screen. Willow heard Jedda's footsteps behind her and then heard his voice over her shoulder.

"Who is that?" he asked in a hushed voice.

"I-I know him," Willow stuttered, pushing past Betty and out onto the porch. She closed the door behind her, indicating some privacy was in order.

"Brad, what are you doing here?" she asked.

"There some trouble here, Willow?" Betty ignored the closed door and stepped out onto the creaky floorboards on the porch, folding her arms over her chest. Willow saw Jedda standing just on the other side of the screen, peering out as he attempted to figure the scene out.

"No, Betty, no trouble. This is Brad and he was just leaving."

"That's not very hospitable," Brad said, taking a seat on the porch swing, flopping down so heavily that the springs sounded like they might snap. "Aren't you Southerners known for your warm welcomes?" he asked smugly, lounging back comfortably.

"No," Betty said with a forced smile. "We're known for our lax laws on shooting unwelcomed guests."

"Feisty," Brad grinned, pointing over at Betty as he winked at Willow. "No need to shoot me. I'm here to talk to Willow, and if she gives me what I want, I'll be on my way."

"And if she don't, then I can shoot you?" Betty asked, raising a threatening eyebrow.

"Betty," Willow said, taking in a deep breath, "would you give us just a minute? I promise he'll be gone."

Betty eyed the boy and bit at her lip as she decided. "I'll be inside loading my shotgun. That ain't an expression either. I mean that very literally. If I don't like what I hear or see out here I won't hesitate to use it."

When Betty stepped through the doorway, Willow watched as she tugged Jedda into the kitchen with her.

"Brad, get out of here."

"Shut the hell up," Brad hissed through clenched teeth as he jumped to his feet. "Did you get my message? The assault charges were dropped. Did you really think you could go to the police and screw up my life? My dad took care of it within two days. You're just lucky it didn't hit the news."

"Great. You win. So go."

"No, you see it doesn't work like that. You want to be a tough girl and try to screw me over, now I don't trust you. I was willing to let you go, figuring you'd be too smart or too scared to ever try anything dumb, but now I know differently. I want your laptop. I know what you have on there and I want it."

"No. I'm keeping it. It's my insurance policy. If you do anything else to me, I'll make sure that everything on it gets to the police and there won't be a thing in the world your dad can do to get you out of that mess." Willow's insides were trembling. Where the courage to say this was coming from, she wasn't sure. She knew crossing Brad was dangerous, but this was her Hail Mary move, her last stand. He needed to know she could bring him down, and she hoped that knowledge would be enough to get him to leave her alone.

"Are you stupid? Do you really think that's how this is going to go down? You're going to blackmail me?"

“I’m not blackmailing you. I’m telling you if you leave me alone, I’ll never do anything with it.”

“Yeah, I’m going to trust a bitch like you. Some filthy street trash that was trying to pass herself off as something better. Something I’d actually date. You made a fool of me in front of all my friends. My father was furious when he found out who you really were. Think about the shame you’re bringing to your parents. Not those dirtbags your brother killed, I mean the people who adopted you, and then this? You’re disgusting. You and your crazy ass brother belong together. I knew if I found him I’d find you,” Brad spat as he leaned over Willow and pointed down into her face. “Now give me what I came here for, or I’ll go in there and get it myself.”

“No,” Willow said, her voice cracking regardless of how hard she tried to steady herself. She felt Brad’s bear-like hands clamp down on both her biceps and his fingers pushed painfully on the bruises that hadn’t healed from last time.

“You really need me to beat the shit out of you twice?”

“Get your fucking hands off her.” Jedda barreled out the door with his fist pulled back to strike.

“Jedda,” Betty shouted as she cocked her shotgun, stepping out behind him. “I’m just as likely to shoot you before I let you lay a hand on him and end up back in jail. I’ve got this covered, you just step aside.” Betty raised the gun to her shoulder and walked straight up to Brad, placing the barrel at his ribs and digging in. “I suggest you let her go and step the hell off my porch before I spray your guts all over the place.”

“You’re a fucking psycho,” Brad hissed at Betty as he forcefully released Willow and pushed her back.

"Well hello, pot, I'm the kettle, and you're black as coal. Now get the hell off my porch, and if I ever get a glimpse of you back here you won't get a warning."

Brad backed down the porch slowly and moved toward his BMW parked sideways in the driveway.

"I can get to you, Willow. I can get to you anywhere. You're not safe here," Brad said as he pointed a threatening finger at her.

Betty turned the barrel of her gun toward the back of the shiny car and squeezed the trigger. The pop made Willow scream and cover her ears. It was a sound she hadn't heard since the day Jedda killed their parents. The shot peppered the back of the car, pinging against the metal and breaking the glass of the taillights.

"What the hell?" Brad yelled, ducking down and covering his head with his hands.

"I can get you, Brad. I can get you anywhere. You're not safe here," Betty parroted back as she rested the gun against her side.

Brad quickly surveyed the damage to the back of his car, let some more expletives escape his mouth and then fell into the front seat before slamming his foot on the gas. A spray of dirt and rock kicked up behind him as he fishtailed out of the long dirt driveway.

Willow still had her hands over her ears as she shook with fear. She wasn't sure who was more frightening, Betty or Brad. But it made her glad that at least one of them was on her side.

"Go in the house, you two. Call Michael and Bobby. I've got a feeling things are about to get exciting around here again."

Chapter Six

The porch was once again loaded with what Jedda was beginning to consider the regulars. All of them perched in their seats staring at Willow and him. The only new guest was a four legged one. Bruno, the big German Shepard that belonged to Piper and Bobby, had come along with them tonight. Maybe for extra protection; he certainly looked capable of it. As Betty recounted the afternoon's events, all eyes suddenly turned toward her, and Jedda considered the shift in attention a welcomed relief.

"You shot at his car?" Bobby asked, his voice octaves higher than normal as he tried to understand the situation.

"I felt the boy needed a more tactile message to drive home what I was saying. This wasn't some bratty college kid trying to look like a tough guy. In my humble opinion he's off his damn rocker and hell bent on causing this girl harm."

"It's not a big deal," Willow shrugged, folding her arms over her chest and staring down the driveway.

"Roll up your sleeves," Betty insisted, practically doing it herself before Willow acquiesced. The whole room gasped at the sight of dark purple bruises that dotted their way from her wrists up to her shoulders. "I haven't checked out the rest of her, but I'm guessing it doesn't stop there."

"What the hell, Willow?" Bobby demanded, slamming his hand down on the small coffee table. "Why didn't you tell me? I'm a goddamn cop. I can help you . . . Jesus."

"Unless you're praying over there, Bobby, let's try not to bring the Son of God into this," Betty warned as she took a seat next to Willow.

"There are cops up in New York, and they certainly couldn't help me," Willow snapped as she yanked her sleeves back down.

"And how about we don't yell at the poor girl either, Bobby. She's the victim here. It's not as easy as you think to ask for help in these types of situations," Piper said, putting her hand on Bobby's shoulder and giving him a look to ease up.

"Right," Jules chimed in. "Being in an abusive relationship isn't as straight forward as you guys would like to believe."

"Can you all stop talking about me like I'm not here?" Willow shot up and paced across the porch, looking like a wild animal in a much-too-small cage. "I'm not in an abusive relationship, and I'm not a victim. You don't understand the situation, so please stop trying to figure this out."

"Willow, we don't understand the situation," Jedda said, stepping in front of his sister and forcing her with his body to stop moving around. "So you need to tell us. Tell us so we can help you. What happened and why is he here? What does he want?"

"Why is he here?" Willow asked, her eyes flashing with anger. "He's here because of you." She pushed back hot tears that were threatening to stream down her face. "All these bruises are because of you." She gestured down to her arms and then shoved Jedda backward, though he barely moved.

"Start explaining yourself now. I've got one priority here and that's to make sure Jedda stays safe and out of prison. I'm not going to let you get in the way of that," Michael, who'd been quiet up until this point, said.

Willow ignored Michael's words and directed her answer back at her brother. "Your crusade to free yourself from prison worked out perfectly for everyone but me. I was living my life. I had friends and a school I loved. I had a boyfriend who was fast-tracked to become partner at his father's law firm after he passed the bar. We had plans. That is until I went from being Willow, the girl with an impressive pedigree who grew up on the beach and had a bright future in music, to Willow, the orphaned sister of a murderer."

"You told him?" Jedda asked, not grasping the depth of Willow's anger.

"I didn't tell him," she shouted, running her fingers through her hair in sheer exasperation. "The news took care of that for me. Right in the middle of a dinner with a bunch of his colleagues, which was so convenient. Everyone's phone starts chirping with breaking news and, boom, there is my face next to a story that's more fiction than truth. Painting me as some kind of filthy, damaged, sex-trafficking victim. And just like that the life I was building crumbled. Brad and I left right away and he flew off the handle. Can you blame him?"

"Yes," Betty, Jules, and Piper said in unison. "You bet your ass I blame him," Betty continued. "There ain't never a reason in the world to raise your hand to a woman. And it looks like he did a hell of a lot more than just slap you around."

"Yes, he did. He lost it. Beat the shit out of me. And I did the right thing, the adult thing. I went to the police. I went through the degrading process of them taking pictures of my body from every angle. Measuring my bruises. I did what I was supposed to do and all for nothing because apparently his father had it thrown out and made it look as though it never happened."

The steely tone in Michael's voice was gone now as he stepped toward the corner of the porch where Willow had taken refuge. "There are things we can do. I don't care who he is, we have contacts of our own and we can get the charges brought back against him."

"Hell no." Willow folded her arms over her chest and stared up into his face. "You don't know what these people are capable of. I'm done."

Piper, who was staring off into the tree line, seemed to be working something out in her head.

"Wait a second, if the charges were dropped why is he here? That doesn't make any sense. He won, why come down here?"

"He wants something else from her," Betty said, not looking like she gave a crap that this meant she was eavesdropping on the girl.

"You were listening to my conversation?" Willow shot angrily.

"It's a good thing I was or I think you'd be looking at a few more bruises this evening."

"Willow, cut the crap and tell us what he wants," Michael demanded, letting his intolerance and annoyance return. "You're not taking into consideration the impact this could have on your brother. If he gets mixed up in anything like this he could get tossed back in prison for even the smallest infraction."

Willow's eyes drew down to her shoes and she bit at her lip, looking torn by indecision. "He wants my laptop. I have some stuff on it that would incriminate him in . . . something. Something his father couldn't get him out of.

Because I went to the police he doesn't trust me now, and he wants it back."

"So give it to him," Jules said pointing at the door. "Go in there and get it and give it back to him. Get rid of him."

"That won't get rid of him. He's got a drug problem, and he's not stable right now. Even if I give it to him now he'll spin out about it eventually and think I made copies or told someone. There is no turning back at this point. That's why I need to get on a bus and go somewhere he can't find me."

"You just got here, don't you want to be here with me?" Jedda asked, like he'd just caught an arrow through the heart. "We've already lost so much time together. You're going to leave school and your parents? You're actually considering that? You can't run away."

"I can't go back to school. If you knew how everyone was looking at me, you'd understand. My parents . . . they'll be better off if I go. They never told anyone my history, what had happened to me, what you did. People will be all over them. They must be so embarrassed. I just need to go." Willow's lip curled and her chin quivered as the tears started to fall.

Every eye went to Piper who was fighting back her own tears now as she crossed the porch and joined Michael at Willow's side.

"You don't stand a chance if you leave," Piper insisted. "I've been right where you are. I've run before. I can tell you from personal experience there isn't a safer place in the world than right here. If you go, he will find you. Maybe not right away, but if he's set on it, eventually he'll get to you. And every day he doesn't, you'll feel like a prisoner in your own skin. You'll spend more time looking over your shoulder than you do living your life. The only difference between him finding you somewhere out there rather than you staying here is out there you won't have a cop who cares about you. No lawyer working in your corner. No brother. No friends. And most importantly, no Betty with a shotgun. There is nothing lonelier and more dangerous than walking off this porch and running."

Jedda felt his hands ball into fists at the thought of his sister out alone in the world. The marks on her arms brought him back to those days when their parents would hurt them. He'd given up everything, changed his life forever, so Willow would never have to suffer again, but it hadn't worked. She didn't look happy and carefree, and she certainly didn't seem safe. He felt an anger building inside him that was too familiar for his liking. His fierce need to protect his sister was something that had been etched into his soul and though he'd had many years to let that mark fade, it was burning hot right now.

"Where is this guy now?" Jedda asked, the blood rushing to his face.

"Jedda," Michael said, resting his hand on his shoulder and giving him a small shake, "we're not hunting him down. We're going to be logical about this and come up with a solution that keeps everyone safe."

"Look at her arms," Jedda pleaded as he moved back toward Willow. "The damage is already done, she wasn't safe."

"Don't talk about me in the third person. I'm not a child anymore. I'm not starving and helpless. I don't need that kind of help again. I don't want it. I want to leave here and get as far away from Brad as I possibly can until he moves on to something else or gets locked up for doing something stupid." Willow's hands were flailing as she spoke frantically.

"Let us help you," Piper begged as she tried to calm Willow with a gentle touch of her hand. Bruno sidled up to them both, lending his own type of quiet support. "Let us make sure if he ever plans to put his hands on you again he has to go through everyone on this porch to do it. We'll get a restraining order. We'll put the police here in Edenville on notice. We'll buy some time while we try to figure out what to do with the laptop and the information on it. These guys might be powerful, but we've been up against this stuff before. And you know what?"

"What?" Willow asked hesitantly, the smallness of her voice ripping Jedda's guts out.

"We've won every time. Every single time."

Chapter Seven

"She's in good hands," Betty said as she slid another spatula full of scrambled eggs onto the plate in front of Jedda. "Michael will make sure she's safe while they talk to the police and file the restraining order. I know it's hard to sit back and let other people help, but that's what friendship is all about."

"Thanks, Betty. I know he's looking out for her. All of you are. It's just so quiet here and my mind keeps going to that guy. That bastard putting his hands on her. It just brings me right back to when we were kids and I . . ." Jedda felt his hand closing tightly around his glass of orange juice.

"Don't go busting that glass, it's one of my favorites," she said as she took it from his hand and moved to the sink to soak the dishes. "I know watching people we love get hurt is like torture, but she ain't getting hurt anymore. Not while I'm around. Not while any of us are. You just have to trust. You just have to."

As he shoveled another forkful of egg into his mouth, chasing it with a strip of bacon, Jedda tried to let an image of these people form in his mind. He pictured them with linked arms, surrounding Willow in protection.

"Well at least you haven't lost your appetite," Betty sang as she crossed the room, two more strips of bacon ready for him.

"I'm going to work out this morning so I want to make sure I have a lot of fuel to burn off."

"I think there might be some weights that belonged to Stan out in the shed. They'd be buried under all the stuff I've got out there, so you'd get a workout just trying to find them. What else do you do, like jumping jacks or something?"

"The one thing you have a lot of time for in prison is exercise. I was benching about three hundred pounds and I did a lot of boxing. Not against anyone else, just a bag, but it was a good work out."

"There's one of those out there too, I think," Betty said, lighting up with excitement. "Anything in there is up for grabs."

Jedda took the last bite of his breakfast and headed for the door. This was part of what he'd been missing since he left prison and he was anxious to start sweating again, and if there was a punching bag in there, it would hopefully help him work out some of the overwhelming desire to beat the hell out of Brad.

He pulled open the heavy doors of the left leaning shed and coughed as a puff of dust rose to his face. Waving it away he stepped inside and took in his surroundings. There were stacks of boxes pushed against the walls and stray lawn equipment down by his feet. As he peered deeper into the shed he saw the leathery red material of a punching bag and the shiny metal bar of a weight bench. He felt a small piece of his anger slide away, and he knew this was the right thing for him.

It took forty minutes to shift things around in the shed enough to be able to rehang the punching bag and set up the weight bench, which was a little rickety. He slipped his hands into the old gloves and sucked in a deep breath before slamming his fists into the heavy red bag. It was, as he hoped, more calming than anything he'd done since leaving prison. The rhythmic clanking of the chain as he let loose was like music to his ears. He felt his knuckles begin to ache and he knew the skin that had softened slightly over the last week, was breaking. He didn't care though, it felt too good to stop. The sweat that was pouring down from his head ran into his eyes, but he didn't wipe it away. He moved his feet, back and forth like a dance, feeling the dirt floor of the shed shifting below him.

When his body could physically take no more, he dropped heavily to the weight bench and rested his head on the slight cushion of his boxing gloves. His body was coursing with energy, his blood pulsing its way through his body. When he caught his breath again, he stood, but a lightness in his head had him grabbing the closest thing for support. He leaned on a box that quickly gave way under his weight, and the contents spilled everywhere.

On the floor lay a pile of newspaper articles, a few books with titles Jedda didn't recognize, and a white robe. As he picked up the clippings from the paper, it took him a moment to realize what the headlines meant. Klan surges in response to civil rights, and New leadership strengthens the Klan. Bombing, beatings, and cross burnings increase.

Jedda picked up a few of the tattered paperback books, their titles all linked to the Klu Klux Klan, one more insulting and bigoted than the last. A framed picture, with the glass cracked, lay down by his feet. As he lifted it he pushed the dust off so he could get a better look. A man standing in his Klan robe, his white hat removed so his proud face could be seen. Next to him was a small gangly girl with pigtails and a solemn-looking woman.

Why any of this stuff was out here confused the hell out of Jedda. Betty seemed to be the most tolerant and accepting person he'd met in his life and she certainly didn't come across as racist. As he leaned over to place the photo back in the box he heard a quiet voice.

"That's my daddy there. Doesn't he look so proud?" Betty asked as she tucked her hands into her pockets and leaned against the doorframe of the shed.

"I'm sorry, the box fell over. I wasn't going through everything," Jedda apologized as he replaced the photo in the box and leaned down to pick up the books.

"He does look proud though doesn't he?" Betty asked again.

"He does." Jedda agreed, uncomfortably.

"That's me and my mama standing next to him. We don't look quite as proud do we?"

"No," he said, shaking his head as he put the remaining items back in the box.

"When the civil rights movement started I was very young. My first memory of it was when, on a hot summer day, I ran to a water fountain to get a drink, pulled myself up on a stool, and heard my mother scream as though she was on the verge of being murdered. She yanked me by my ponytail and told me that water wasn't for me. It was dirty water. I remember thinking why on earth would they let dirty water come up there. Shouldn't there be a sign? Obviously as I got older I realized there was a sign. Just a different kind of sign. It took me years to realize who my father was and what he was doing to people all in the name of purity and holiness. It's a shame I carry with me every day."

"You shouldn't be ashamed of what he did. You were a kid," Jedda said, taking a seat again on the weight bench.

"Unfortunately it's not always easy to sort out how you feel about things that happened when you're young. You get a little twisted up in what you could control and what is your fault. You worry that some of that is inside of you. There is a lot of guilt when you stood by and did nothing."

"You do a lot now."

"I try to."

"Why keep the box?" Jedda asked, feeling like maybe his question was too bold.

"It's a reminder of how close hate is to all of us. It's around every corner, and if you forget it's there, you're quick to let it in your heart. But with reminders like that, I never lose sight of who I don't want to be. Who I will never become. But there are still days I beat myself up for what happened in and around my home when I was young."

"Do you think that's what Willow is doing?" Jedda asked, making the connection. "Do you think she feels guilty for what happened, for what I did?"

"I'm a very good reader of people. I pride myself on understanding the many layers of the human condition, but your sister is a mystery to me. Why did she come here when she was in trouble? I would think because she knows you would protect her. So then, why does she want to run away so quickly now? She's got everything a child could ask for—good parents, lots of opportunities—but she gets mixed up with a guy like Brad. I kept asking myself, why is she so confusing to me? Then it hit me, because that's what she is, confused. I can't figure her out because she can't figure herself out. I thought back to a time in my life when I felt that way. And I thought of that box right there."

"What can I do for her? She has nothing to feel guilty about. She didn't do anything wrong. Should I tell her that?"

"There's nothing anyone can tell her to change her mind. It's a place she needs to come to on her own."

"How did you get there? How did you stop being confused?"

"I took control of my own life. I stopped beating myself up about it and decided the best thing I could do was be a person who could make a difference. I'd love everyone. I wouldn't judge people, I'd give them a chance. And every time I do that, I heal a little bit. I am not responsible for my father's actions. Understanding that changed my life."

Jedda nodded his head as he struggled to understand what Willow might be feeling. Betty pulled a towel from her shoulder and tossed it over to him.

"Clean up and I'll get you a drink. We can chat more on the porch for a bit."

As Betty disappeared from the doorway Jedda sat quietly for a moment, staring at the box filled with hate. He hadn't realized his sister might be struggling; it was easy to see that the trouble with Brad would be troubling her, but maybe it was deeper.

As he stood to leave he heard a car pulling into the driveway, rumbling over the popping gravel. He walked to the door of the shed but hesitated when he didn't recognize the car.

He watched as Betty stepped out on the porch with her shotgun hanging in her hand. The car door swung open and, much to Jedda's surprise, out stepped a familiar face. He held his breath as he watched Crystal swing her door closed. He saw the streaks of her blonde hair catching the sun and glistening back at him. She walked confidently toward the house with a beaming smile, the smile that always made his heart jump, but then she stopped suddenly. He could hear the words from his hiding spot in the shed, and though his mind was telling him to go to her, his body was motionless.

"Is that a gun?" Crystal asked, stumbling back slightly, her eyes turning from bright cheery slits that complimented her smile to wide and frightened.

"That's how I greet unannounced strangers showing up on my door. Now who sent you here?"

"I'm a friend of Jedda's. My name is Crystal," she answered, instinctively raising her hands into the air.

"That's funny, he's never mentioned you before, Crystal," Betty said, lowering the gun to her side but keeping an unwelcoming stance.

Jedda watched as a look of wounded disappointment crept across Crystal's tired face. "He hasn't mentioned me at all?" she asked, lowering her hands and biting at her thumbnail nervously. "Are you sure?"

Betty seemed to read the same change in expression, and her empathy kicked in. "Well, things have been crazy round here, and he's a quiet guy. Now how did you say you know him?"

"I'm sorry. I shouldn't have come. I was worried, but I can see he has all the protection he needs. I should go." At the sight of Crystal turning on her heels to leave, Jedda's body caught up with his mind. He made his way across the yard quickly as Crystal reached her car.

"Wait," he shouted, his voice cracking with nerves. "Crystal, don't go."

"Jedda," she said, not making a move to come back toward him, her hand still on the handle of her car door. "I hadn't heard from you. Which now I guess I should have taken as a hint."

"I'm sorry. Some stuff came up with my sister and I've just been trying to keep my head straight about it. Did you come down here just to check on me? What about work, did you get time off?"

"I got a lot of time off. I got fired," Crystal choked out, her cheeks going red, clearly not comfortable with the reality of her statement yet.

"Why?" he asked. He didn't want to let himself be distracted by the ache in Crystal's eyes but he felt himself being pulled toward her.

"Because of you I think. After my boss fired me I went out to my car and there was a note on my windshield. Something along the lines of needing to choose my friends better next time and that some things aren't worth the trouble. It implied that you'd be back in prison soon. I assumed it was a message someone wanted me to deliver to you, so I came. Michael had given me the address so I could write you and keep in touch. I guess it was presumptuous of me to come down here. I could have just called and told Michael what happened." Crystal kicked at a rock with the toe of her boot and stared down at the ground. Jedda knew he could swoop in here. Tell her she was right for coming and take away the blanket of embarrassment that she was caught under. But he hesitated.

"Maybe Michael can help you get your job back. They can't fire you just for being nice to me. That's not legal, I'm sure." Jedda knew what he was saying was not enough; he knew Crystal was here for more, hoping he would have been happier to see her. He was happy, but showing her that would only lead her on.

"I don't want my job back. I'm a grown-up. I have a savings account. Practically every major city in the country has a courthouse. Finding another job won't be difficult. But I won't work for a person who finds it so easy to fire an employee of nine years just because someone is pulling the strings. I'll be fine. I'm going to head out though." Crystal pulled her car door open and waved an awkward goodbye.

"Just a minute there, Crystal," Betty said, grabbing a basket from the corner of the porch and racing down the stairs toward the car. "Will you do me a favor before you go? You see that path down there, to the left of that big oak?"

"Yes." Crystal nodded.

"Can you go on down there about two hundred yards or so and pick me some wild flowers? I need them for my table tonight for dinner and these old knees just aren't made for gardening any more. I'm not picky about what you bring back." Betty shoved the basket into Crystal's arms and closed her car door for her. Before the shock could turn to questions, Betty made her way back to the porch.

"You have any change in your pockets?" she asked Jedda who now matched Crystal's look of disbelief and uncertainty.

"No."

Betty dug into her pocket and pulled out a couple of quarters and slapped them into Jedda's hand. "Go with the girl. Stop being an idiot."

"What are the quarters for?" Jedda asked as he heard the heavy front door that was almost always open slammed in his face. He stared at it for a long moment, hoping Betty might be back out to explain what the hell she was talking about. But when she didn't reappear he turned to find Crystal.

"I'm getting flowers?" she asked, gesturing down to the basket.

"And I'm going with you." He shrugged and they both smiled at the peculiar circumstance of this mission.

They headed down behind the house, past the oak, just as Betty had instructed. The path was overgrown to the point where they could only pass through single file. Jedda walked out ahead of Crystal, holding the wiry branches that were just starting to bud with the spring heat. He pinned them back long enough to ensure they didn't slap into her face.

"Do you really think there are flowers back here? Its just woods," Crystal wondered out loud, ducking to avoid a low hanging limb.

"I don't know. I've only been here a few days and I don't really have a good handle on everyone. Betty is special; she seems to care about people, like she's always trying to help even when it just looks like she's butting in."

"Oh, so you think she just didn't want me to leave? She wanted us alone in the woods together?" Crystal asked, stumbling over a rock and slamming into Jedda's back. "Sorry." She grabbed his shoulders to steady herself and the smell of her familiar lotion made him want to turn and kiss her.

"You all right?" he asked, turning and offering his hand. Before she could answer her eyes grew wide and she pointed over her shoulder.

"Holy cow," she whispered.

"Is it a bear?" Jedda asked freezing and hunching his shoulders over like he might be mauled at any minute.

"No look, a clearing and it's full of wild flowers." She pushed past him and walked out into the open field that seemed to stretch forever. It was dotted with the brightest purple and yellow blooms. Off to the left was a loosely stacked ring of stones with a wood roof built up over the top of it.

"Is that a wishing well?" Crystal asked, moving toward it without any hesitation.

"Be careful. It looks like it's about to fall over. Don't get too close."

"Jedda, if you never get close to anything you never get a good enough look to know if it's magic."

"You think that thing is magic? Like a leprechaun is about to jump out and grant you a wish?"

"No, but if I had any coins, I'd sure as hell throw one in. Just in case."

Jedda reached into his pocket and pulled out the two quarters Betty had handed to him. That woman was a puppet master. Frighteningly good. He jogged up to Crystal's side and placed one of the coins in her hand. "Here, now you can make a wish," he said, gesturing to the well.

"What about you, aren't you going to toss one in?"

"I've done a lot of wishing in my life, I think I'd do better to keep my quarter."

"Suit yourself." She shrugged as she peeked her head down into the dark opening of the well. "Hello," she called and smiled when the echo of her voice reverberated around her. She closed her eyes, held the quarter tight in her hands, pressed it over her heart, and then dropped it down the well.

"Which flowers should we pick?" Jedda asked, looking out over the open field. "I don't know what goes together."

"They're wild flowers, that's the beauty of them. They all go together," Crystal answered as she knelt down and began plucking stems topped with all different colors and placing them gently into the basket. "We should get them back to Betty." Crystal averted her eyes from Jedda's.

"Why did you really come down here?" Jedda asked, dropping down to sit beside her. "You got in your car and drove all the way down here. Is there something else going on?"

She hung her head and stopped pulling the flowers, rolling from her knees to a sitting position. "I was really worried about you, but that isn't the only reason I came. I've never had a lot of friends and when you left, I missed you. But hopping in the car and coming down here was not the right thing. You hadn't called. I should have taken the hint. Once we get these flowers back to Betty, I'm going to head home."

"That isn't what I want, you to leave now. I'm just . . ."

"What, Jedda? Talk to me," Crystal begged, touching Jedda's hand gently. "You never had any trouble opening up to me before."

"I'm in a goddamn tailspin here," he huffed, pulling his hand back and running it aggressively through his hair. "People in this town think I'm a monster, but I'm sure that would be the same anywhere I go. There's no running from this thing. My sister, she just shows up here and she's in trouble. This guy, he beat the crap out of her because the news media put up a picture of her and linked her to my release. Completely outed her and what we went through. This dirt bag is some kind of stuck-up spoiled kid and he didn't like that he was dating a 'piece of trash,' in his opinion. And I just can't get myself out of this place where I want to . . . I want to find him."

"Is she hurt?"

"She's banged up and he's not even done with her. He followed her here. He came right to that house and put his hands on her again. He's not going to leave her alone. If you could have seen him, the craziness in his eyes." He clenched his bruised hands into fists as the memory flashed through his mind. "I'm losing it here, Crystal. I want to track the kid down and . . . and . . ."

"Take a breath, Jedda," Crystal insisted, moving to his side and putting her arm around him.

"What if they were wrong about me? What if letting me out was the wrong thing to do and I'm going to hurt someone again? Most people out here think letting me out was a mistake. That I have this evil inside me. Right now I'm not sure I would disagree with them."

"Wanting to hurt someone for beating up your sister doesn't exactly put you in the category of monster. I don't even think it puts you in the minority of the general population. I'd be more worried if you weren't angry."

"There's a difference between angry and what I'm feeling. I can't describe it, but it's scaring the shit out of me."

"Then why are you pushing me away? Maybe I can help you, but you don't seem like you want me here. Let me be here for you."

"Crystal, it isn't that I don't want you here, I just don't want to put you through hell for no reason. You don't deserve that. I'm not—"

"Don't tell me you're no good for me. That's so cliché. Don't give me that line. This isn't some old black and white movie. I'm not some dame who doesn't know what she needs in her life."

"I wasn't going to say that; I was going say I'm no good for anyone, not just you. I don't have anything to offer."

"Bullshit. Jedda, you're compassionate, you're smart and well-read. You've endured incredible things and still stayed positive. Those are parts of your character. They are parts of who you are. I'm not saying that I think you should jump into a relationship, not with me, not with anyone, but I'd like to stick around in case you find yourself ready one day. I want to help you get through this part of your life. Right now, I want to be your friend." Crystal pulled a few more flowers from the earth, more forcefully than she probably realized, and tossed them down into the basket.

"Why? I'm likely going to either screw this up and end up back in jail or, even if I manage not to do that, there is a very good chance I'll never be ready for a relationship. Why would you stick around and take that risk? The odds are you'll get your heart broken."

Crystal put her cool soft hand to Jedda's cheek. "Because that means there is a slim chance that won't happen. There's a sliver of hope my heart will turn out just fine."

"That's enough for you?"

"Yes, because I'm the type of girl who throws coins in wishing wells and believes my wish might actually come true. I drive all night to get to someone who I'm not sure even wants to see me. And I wait around, offer my support, even if nothing ever comes of it. That's just who I am."

Jedda reached down to the basket, pulled a purple violet out, and brought it to his nose. “I don’t want to disappoint you. I don’t want to hurt you or anyone else, but I feel like I’m going to. And I’m not just talking about breaking hearts. I don’t know how to control this feeling. Willow—having her here, it does something to me.”

“Right now, the only thing that would hurt me is if you told me to go back home. So don’t. I’ll try to help you with the rest.”

“And what, you’re just going to be here for me? Like to talk to or whatever?”

“Yes, or whatever. The same way I was back in New York. We were talking about everything. Your parents and everything you remember about them. I’ll listen if you need me to. If I can help with your sister I will. There is nothing up there for me. With my job gone, I just want to see you get through this. I believe in what the court did for you, and I believe you deserve it. I want to be here when you start believing it too. I want to be your friend.”

“Just my friend?” Jedda asked rubbing his thumb across the silky skin of Crystal’s cheek fighting the urge to kiss her soft peach-colored lips.

“If you’re ever ready for more, then you just have to let me know.” She dropped her head and turned her face away from him. He imagined it wasn’t easy for her to put herself out there the way she had. But that was what he admired about her. One of the many things he respected about her. She was unafraid. Unabashedly willing to love.

“We should get these flowers back to Betty before she comes looking for us,” Jedda said as he swept a wind-blown lock of her hair behind her ear. He wanted her. It would be easy to lean in and kiss her, losing himself in that moment. A part of him wanted to be more than friends with her, but he was still convinced in the end she'd be worse off if anything ever happened between them.

"Hopefully she's put that shotgun away," Crystal jested, heading back onto the path and toward the house.

"Trust me, when push comes to shove, Betty's the kind of person you're glad is on your side," Jedda said, jogging up behind Crystal and taking the basket of flowers from her hand. "And wait until you try her biscuits."

Chapter Eight

Michael's somber face as he walked up the driveway of Betty's house was enough to suck the air right out of Jedda's lungs. Something hadn't gone right, that much was obvious. Willow didn't look particularly happy either, but she hadn't since she arrived, so that was no change. A pang of guilt spread across his chest. Here he was enjoying the company of a friend, laughing and sipping lemonade, while his sister was fighting for her safety. And judging by their expressions, she was losing.

Bobby, Piper, and Jules had come in a few minutes before them and politely welcomed Crystal to Edenville. Clay had come home from preparing for the restaurant renovations. The house was buzzing with noise now, but, at the sight of Michael and Willow approaching, a hush fell over them.

"How'd it go?" Bobby asked as he handed a cold beer over to Michael.

"Not bad. Could be better, but we're not completely out of options. We just need to adjust the plan a bit." Michael paused at the sight of their newest guest. "Hey, Crystal, I didn't expect to see you down here."

"It's a long story. You go ahead and tell yours first," she said, waving a hello to Willow who uneasily waved back.

"We requested a restraining order but didn't get it. They didn't see the threat as imminent enough, and since the report regarding the original attack was completely redacted there was no way to show prior violence. We fought it pretty hard but they wouldn't budge. They said they'd keep an eye out for Brad in town, and if he threatens or causes bodily harm to her from this point on, we'd have no problem getting a protection order." Michael spun the top off the beer and took a long swig.

Betty rested her hands on her hips and kicked her head to the side as though she must have misheard something. "Isn't a restraining order there to keep something like that from happening? Why would you need him to hurt her again in order to get the paper that says he needs to stay away? That's so crooked you could hide it behind a corkscrew. Why do they do things like that?"

"That's the million dollar question. It's a flaw in the system, one of many. But the judge wouldn't waver on it. Plus, you know what popular opinion out there is about Jedda; now they see his sister here, bringing with her some trouble. I think they were just looking to stonewall us."

"Who was it, what judge?" Piper asked, offering her seat to Willow, whose legs must have been just tired enough to take it.

"Milton Crosby," Michael replied, taking an even larger swig of his beer, drinking the rest of it down, and then tossing the bottle into the bin by the steps where all the empties went.

"Ugh, I hate him," Betty groaned. "That bucked-toothed, ugly bastard. I swear that man could eat corn on the cob through a picket fence."

"You're full of them tonight, honey," Clay said as he wrapped his arms around Betty, drew her into him, and kissed her lips gently. "Whenever you get angry, you start talking like a crazy woman. I love it."

"Hell, this stuff makes me hopping mad," Betty groaned, though she softened in Clay's arms.

Willow reached for the bottle of wine that was being passed around and poured a glass. "She's right though, he was an ugly son of a bitch. But I didn't expect them to help me anyway. Brad and his father, Thomas Angelo, aren't people you can get restraining orders against."

"So what's next?" Jules asked as she lowered herself into a chair and adjusted a pillow behind her back, trying unsuccessfully to get comfortable.

"We wait. Hopefully Brad moves on, and his threats are just empty bullying," Michael said, nodding as he tried to assure everyone.

"And we'll all be here with you in the meantime." Bobby clanked his beer bottle against Willow's wine glass in a sign of solidarity, but it seemed to do nothing for Willow's confidence. Jedda searched his mind for a moment. Over the last two days had he seen his sister smile, or talk about a friend, or share a happy memory? Perhaps it was his own fault for building up an idea of what reuniting with her would be like, but so far he felt only worry for her.

As much as he didn't want to add to the weight of the situation, he knew Michael needed to stay up to date. "We can't be sure, but I think Crystal getting fired yesterday might have something to do with Brad. Someone left her this note." Jedda passed the paper over to Michael and watched as his jaw tensed and he swallowed hard.

"Fired?" Michael asked, seeming genuinely shocked at the idea of someone as efficient and hard-working as Crystal being fired.

"Seriously?" Willow huffed. "Did Brad seriously do that? I knew it. I knew this would be like six degrees of separation, slowly dismantling shit around me. Hurting anyone who has any sort of tie to me. He's not going to just stop."

"I'm sorry this happened, Crystal." Michael tucked the paper into his sport coat pocket and gestured for Bobby to toss him another beer from the cooler.

Crystal pulled her silky corn-colored hair into a ponytail and shrugged her shoulders. "Don't be sorry. It was only a job. I can get another one. I'm more worried about what you want to do to take care of this guy. I'm worried for both Willow and Jedda, who's an easy target at this point. You know how little it would take to get him put back in jail."

"There's nothing we can do. You guys don't know him like I do. He won't stop." Willow drained her wine glass with a large swig, wincing as she drank it all down.

Michael lounged back in his chair and crossed his legs. "Everybody has an Achilles' heel. Even Thomas and Brad Angelo. We just need to find it. There's always a way to take people down. I need a little time to figure out their weaknesses. I've already started doing research. We can win this."

"Why not use the information you have on the laptop? You said you have evidence of a crime his father couldn't get him out of. Why not bring it to a district attorney?" Piper asked.

"I thought about it until I started digging into this firm. It's the same reason we didn't turn over Judge Lions for the original wrong doing. We didn't know who he had in his pocket, and if we show our hand too early or to the wrong people Willow could be in grave danger. These men move the chains all the time, they make the rules."

"They're infamous," Crystal added. "When their firm is involved in a case at my courthouse the chatter is unbelievable. They're known for threatening witnesses, bribing judges, and slandering victims. Their clients are wealthy and so are they. I agree with Michael, it would be risky to try to show your hand this early. You'd be better off seeing if it dies down on its own."

Jules looked longingly at the glass of wine in Willow's hand as she tried to grasp the situation. "So you can't just give him back the evidence because you don't think that will be enough for him to leave you alone. And you can't turn in the evidence because you don't know who you can trust or who is working for this guy. So you're going to do nothing?"

"No," Michael said, shooting Jules an annoyed look. "I'm going to take the laptop and keep it safe while trying to find some other way to deal with them. If we find an ally in this, someone who wants to bring them down more than we do or find some other angle for dealing with them we can do it with far less drama."

"And in the meantime?" Piper asked as she topped off Willow's glass and then her own.

Before anyone else could answer, Betty chimed in with a smile that implied she didn't have a care in the world. That everything was going to be all right. That ability to act perfectly content in the face of trials was one of the gifts she gave the world and, tonight, Jedda appreciated it. "In the meantime," she hummed, "we all need a good distraction. Like a wedding."

Every eye turned toward Jules who was shoveling another handful of crackers into her mouth. "About that," she mumbled, crumbs flying from her mouth before she could catch them. She choked down the dry snack and continued, "Michael and I talked about it. We think it would be better if we held off on the wedding until things settle down. I'm taking all these postponements as a sign that maybe we should wait."

Betty's smile evaporated like steam in the wind. "But all you've been talking about is making sure you say your vows before Françoise makes her appearance in this world."

"Ma, really, still with the Françoise?"

"It's a beautiful name, but don't change the subject. This was very important to you. Are you really telling me you just suddenly had a change of heart?"

"We're trying to be realistic," Jules said, filling her hand with another stack of crackers.

Bobby crossed the porch and sat down next to Jules. "Why? You're never realistic. It seems like a strange time to start."

"Shut up, you ass. No one asked your opinion." Jules shot daggers at him with her eyes. "Sorry," she apologized as she softened her face slightly, "it's the hormones. And that's kind of the point. I'm as big as a house. Every part of me is swollen. My dress is too tight now. Half the people on our guest list wouldn't come anyway because they think we're running some kind of halfway house for the criminally dangerous up here. I can't get any of the catering equipment I wanted. It just seems like a lost cause." Jules's voice broke with emotion and her chin began to quiver. "This isn't how I imagined it and so I don't want it any more," she choked out, now in a full-on blubbering fit.

Michael stood, walked over to her and reached his hand down to lift her to her feet. "I think we better be going for the night. It's usually all downhill from this point." Jules threw herself into Michael's arms and wept heavily into his shoulder.

"I-I'm sorry," she muttered before pressing her face hard into his shirt. "I don't know what's wrong with me. These damn hormones."

"Go on home, child," Betty said, patting her daughter's back. "It ain't your fault. Babies soak up all our good sense when they're in our bellies. You're supposed to be a little crazy. That's how you know you're doing it right."

"Thanks, Ma," Jules croaked as she waved a pitiful goodbye to everyone and Michael helped lower her into the front seat of the car.

As they drove off, the chirping of the crickets and the squeaking of the porch swing were the only sounds. Everyone looked split between stunned and sad. Jedda couldn't help but feel like his presence here was more disruptive then he had hoped. He was bringing trouble and causing problems for everyone. He had the urge to run, to stand up right this minute and head for the main road and never look back. But there was something tethering him to that porch. As he sat on the chair that had been brought out for him, he felt the soft skin of Crystal's arm brushing against his. It was just the subtle byproduct of close quarters, but for a man who'd gone so long without the connection to other people, this small act was enough to keep him from bolting down the steps.

"So should we do it this weekend or next?" Betty asked, pulling her sweater closed against the cool spring night breeze.

"Do what?" Piper asked as she tipped some more wine into her own glass.

"Have a wedding for Michael and Jules. You heard her. She only wants one if she can have it the way she wants. So we'll give her the wedding she was hoping for."

"Like a surprise?" Willow asked skeptically, furrowing her brows and narrowing her eyes.

"Yes, why? Do you think that's too presumptuous of me? Am I butting in too much?" Betty asked, sipping on her tea to hide her small smile and looking as though she didn't care what the answer to that question would be.

"Well, I don't know," Bobby said, sitting back down next to Piper and resting his hands behind his head. "You'd be coining the phrase surprise wedding. That should be telling you something right there. If no one has done it, there is probably a good reason why."

Slapping her hands together and jumping to her feet Betty hooted, "You're right. We'd be pioneers. Fantastic! Now let's split the tasks up here so that we can pull this off. I think next weekend would be better, but it's awful close to her due date. If we did it this weekend we'd only have three days to plan. But on the bright side, we'd have better luck of keeping it a secret that way. Okay, it's settled. We're throwing Michael and Jules a surprise wedding this Sunday."

Willow tipped yet another glassful of wine into her mouth. "So this is a thing?" she asked, looking around at everyone. "You're really doing this?" The slur of a wine-buzz was heavy on her red-stained lips and Jedda wondered if she did this often. If the warm sensation of wine was how she escaped.

"We're doing this sweetie," Betty said as she pulled a notebook from the table next to her. "Now, I'm going to put you down as the wedding singer. Do you know any good love songs?"

"Ha," Willow chuckled, then became serious as she seemed to realize Betty was not making an attempt at humor. "You want me to sing love songs at your surprise wedding for two people who just said they didn't want to get married?"

"I'll put you down for the bride and groom's dance," Betty decided, scratching down some notes.

"But—" Willow started, before Piper waved her off.

"It's like quicksand, Willow, don't fight it or it gets worse. Take the song, and be happy you're not leading the chicken dance or holding a limbo stick."

"I can help with the food," Jedda said, trying to pull the attention from his sister before she said something that might not be easily taken back. "I can cook and serve."

"That would be great," Clay said, patting Betty's leg. "I'll help with the food too, of course. I'll drive out to Sandersville and pick up the equipment if the idiots here in Edenville don't want to rent it to us."

Crystal raised her hand timidly and caught Betty's eye. "This ain't no classroom, cookie, you can talk whenever the mood strikes you."

"I can sew," Crystal said, dropping her hand down quickly. "I'm a decent seamstress, so if you gave me her dress I could let it out without her even knowing."

Jedda felt a twinge of pride rise inside him. Crystal was a good person. She was good just for the sake of being so, and it was nice to have her sitting beside him. She was his friend, his contribution to this group, and it made him happy to know she was fitting in so well. The way she'd hopped in the car and had driven here. The way she'd just volunteered to help a cause that she could have easily avoided. Crystal went the extra mile and always did it with an infectious exuberance. How could you not love that? That was the easy part he realized. Having feelings for her wasn't difficult, figuring out if he was worthy of her feelings toward him was much more of a challenge. He wished the same could be said for Willow.

Piper and Bobby, cuddled together on the swing, exchanged a private look. "We'll take care of the decorations and setting everything up, once you pick a place for it. Any suggestions?"

Crystal raised her hand again, and then dropped it quickly when Betty threw her a look. "Back behind the house, there's this field. It's loaded with wild flowers and this wishing well. If you put an arbor up, cleared the path to make it easier to get to, it would be the most beautiful backdrop for a wedding."

"That's a great idea," Betty sang as she jotted down more notes. "I'll take care of the invites. People are timid of what's going on up here and only our real friends will turn out. That's probably for the best, but I'll try to sway anyone who might be on the fence about it."

Bobby laughed as he spoke, "And I'll start putting away some bail money. I've seen you sway people before."

"No, no, I'll be very diplomatic about it. If they need too much swaying then I don't want them here anyway. And Michael's parents and sister weren't planning to come out until after the baby was born. They couldn't make the trip twice with their schedules. So we won't have to worry about any out-of-town guests."

"My parents were hoping to come, too, but they won't be able to make it on such short notice," Bobby said, shrugging it off. "They're so anxious to see you, Jedda, and to meet Willow. They'll come down once the baby is born."

Jedda smiled at the thought of the Wrights. They were his first real look into what life could be like outside the hell he'd grown up in. They'd visited him regularly in prison over the last year, but he was looking forward to being able to see them out here, where he was free. Normal people take for granted the ability to reach out and hug someone whenever they feel like it. To call them, just because you want to hear their voices. None of that exists in prison. He wanted to interact with them on his terms.

"Willow," Betty said as she made another note, "I'm going to put you down for another song I used to love. Bobby can print the lyrics and such off the interweb."

"The interweb?" Willow grinned, tipping the wine bottle over her glass for the third time. "My computer box doesn't have a microwave signal up here, so that would be a big help."

"Good to hear," Betty smirked. "But just so you know, there is a difference between not knowing the latest tech terms and being too dumb to know when someone is being a smart ass."

Willow's lips pressed shut and her face burned bright red. "Sorry," she whispered, hiding slightly behind her big wine glass.

"It's okay, dear. But now I'm putting you down for two more songs too. Keep it up and you'll have a full playlist to learn."

* * * *

"I'm going back to my hotel," Crystal said as the last embers of the fire began to dim.

"Are you sure?" Jedda asked as he stood and leaned against the rail of the porch. "I hate to have you driving back so late in the dark by yourself."

"The house seems pretty full, and I'm not much of a camper. I don't sleep under the stars."

"There are two couches in the living room. You can have one," Jedda said, looking up at the stars Crystal had just mentioned, trying to look as nonchalant as possible.

"I don't think that's a good idea," Crystal said, fishing her keys out of her purse. "I'm a bit of a werewolf, I think."

"What does that mean?" Jedda asked, assuming it was some trendy phrase he didn't know about yet.

"During the day, it's easier to just be your supportive friend. I remind myself the transition you're going through and how uncomplicated that needs to be. But I'm afraid with the moon out, us curled up on a couple couches, I might forget. I don't want to lose focus on what's important."

"Are you saying you think you'd jump me?" Jedda laughed as he ran his hand over the stubble on his cheek.

"Yes," Crystal said with a deadpan look. "And trust me, you wouldn't be kicking me off your couch either." Crystal ran her hand across his clenched stomach muscles as she moved down the steps of the porch toward her car. "It's better if I go."

"I have a feeling you're right," Jedda whispered in a raspy voice. "But I want you to stay anyway."

Crystal stopped in her tracks and looked back at him like she'd just heard a ghost whispering in her ear. "What do you mean?"

"I can't sleep. I mean, I don't sleep. I know it's a lot to ask, and you'd have to fight off those werewolf tendencies, but the night . . . it's the hardest for me. I was wandering outside last night and a neighbor pulled a gun on me. It's not fair of me to keep you here, to make you be my friend, and only my friend, but the thought of you leaving right now is killing me."

Crystal bit nervously at her lip as she searched Jedda's face for something more. "I was only kidding about coming onto your couch." She smirked. "I have self control for God's sake." She walked back past him, this time not touching him at all and he felt as though he'd been robbed of something.

"Thanks. I'm not sure what I'd do without you."

"Let's hope you never have to find out then." She smiled as she reached her hand out to him. It wasn't the sensual lacing of fingers that two lovers might share, but instead just the encompassing warmth of a friend's touch. Jedda felt equal parts of calm and guilt. Having Crystal with him made him feel like he could make it from sundown to sunup. But on the other hand, every ounce of strength she gave him felt like something he was stealing from her. If Crystal was what made him feel better, what would happen when she realized he wasn't able to do anything for her in return?

They sat on the couches, talking for hours about the world. About all the things he'd missed while he'd been locked up. She tried to give him the short versions of all the advances in technology and all the political changes in the world. Then she turned to something more personal and Jedda felt his stomach drop slightly.

"Have you talked to Willow more about your parents? I wonder what she remembers of them, of that time in her life."

"I'm not sure. She was younger than me, but old enough to remember I'd imagine." Jedda shrugged. He'd talked to Crystal in more depth than he had with anyone else about what he remembered from his younger years.

She made it easy, she asked all the right questions and never seemed to push too hard.

"You'd be amazed what people can push out of their mind when they experience trauma. The brain is capable of doing amazing things to protect itself. I think it would be good for you to talk to her, see where she is with all of it. I'd be happy to be there with you."

"I don't know. This isn't at all the reunion I thought we'd have. Something ridiculous inside me just thought we wouldn't skip a beat. We'd be best friends again and she'd tell me how great her life has been, how much I saved her."

"You did, literally, save her life."

"I know that, and I'm sure she knows that too, but there is something standing between us. Something she isn't saying. I feel like sometimes she's angry with me, other times she's angry with herself. You women are impossible to figure out."

"Hey, that's painting with a bit of a broad brush. I'm sure she just needs more time. As strange as it is for you to be out in this new world, it's probably strange for her to see you back in it. Just keep trying. I think talking about what happened, what you both remember and went through, will be important. I'd give it a try."

"Thanks," Jedda said, finally lying back on the couch and kicking his feet up, his eyes heavy with sleep. "Tell me again about this social media stuff. I still can't understand why people need it. They just write what's going on in their lives? Why? Who do they think is reading it? Who would care about such insignificant things?"

"That's the question of the hour. Is the world really filled with such narcissists that we all believe people will be enthralled with what we ate for breakfast? Sadly the answer to that question so far, seems like a resounding yes." Crystal lay back on her own couch and pulled the blanket up over her. "Good night, Jedda," she whispered as she rolled away from him.

"Good night, Crystal," he said, staring over at her crown of long blonde hair that hung over the side of the couch. "Stay on your own couch." He smirked as he rolled away from her and faced the wall.

"I will," she assured him.

"I was talking to myself."

Chapter Nine

If there was such a thing as torture by socializing, surely Willow was in the midst of it. Following Betty around like an obedient puppy while she recruited wedding guests was like an orchestra of nails down the chalkboard. There were the blatant disparagements against her brother she had to listen to. Then the nosy bastards who wanted as much gossip as their little brains could hold. It was all a test of her thinly worn willpower and she was on the verge of losing it, until she realized where they were headed next. The office of Dr. Josh Nelson, the man who'd helped Jedda. Though she was trying hard to deny it, she was looking forward to making a stop that included a familiar face, and a good-looking one at that.

She sat in the cushioned leather chair next to Betty in Josh's office as they waited for him to finish up with a patient.

"This practice belonged to Josh's father before he retired. Some folks in town think he's too young to have his own office like this, but he's very good at what he does."

"After today I'm starting to realize people in this town have an opinion about everything." Willow shrugged, thinking this conversation with Josh might go exactly as the last five had. Sorry Betty, we just can't make it. We don't feel right about it.

When Josh stepped into his office, Willow's eyes were locked on him. She found herself reluctantly intrigued by his gentle smile. His white coat and hanging stethoscope gave him an air of responsibility and togetherness that reminded her how much a mess her life was.

"A surprise wedding?" Josh asked as he folded his hands and leaned forward on his desk. Willow realized she'd been so caught up in dissecting his features she missed the first half of the conversation. Betty and Josh were chatting and all she could do was check him out. He was not a broad-shouldered man, just average in build, but his face was almost painfully sweet. His half smile and the way he styled his hair, a form of messy that clearly took effort to accomplish, just added to his overall nice guy look. That was it, Willow determined. He looked like a perfectly nice guy. She had wrongly thought that about Brad when they met, but now as she compared the two she could see where she had gone wrong. Brad looked like a lot of things, but none would fall under that nice category. Brad looked polished. He looked confident and important, but now, looking back, it was a cleverly designed disguise. Josh, on the other hand, looked like he didn't have a mean bone in his body, and though he was tall there was nothing intimidating about him.

"Do people do surprise weddings, or is this something you've come up with?" he continued, narrowing his eyes at Betty and drawing Willow's attention away from the dimple at the corner of his mouth and back to the conversation.

"I'm the pioneer of such things," Betty said with an air of pride.

"Yes," Willow said, her exhaustion with the day outweighing her ability to shut her mouth. "She's like the Christopher Columbus of crossing personal boundaries. I think there's a chance they could write a book about it some day."

Josh let out a loud chuckle, but quickly righted himself when he remembered who was the butt of that joke.

"Hmm," Betty hummed as she jotted something down in her wedding notebook. "So looks like you'll be learning the lyrics for another little ditty."

Willow rolled her eyes and flopped back into her chair. "How many more songs do you plan to force me to perform?"

"Punishment by performance. I've always liked your style, Betty," Josh chided, winking at Willow. His bright eyes were an odd mix of gold flecks and amber swirls, and when he flashed them her way it made her accidently bite her tongue.

"So can we expect you there on Sunday?" Betty asked, her pen hovering over her notebook.

"Why the campaign? You're out recruiting wedding guests?" he asked, avoiding the question.

"You know how this town is. People aren't too pleased with my latest houseguest and as a result, some friendships are being tested. I'm sure that's not the case for you, right?" Betty raised an eyebrow at Josh, and Willow found herself silently praying he wasn't that guy. Hoping he wasn't the kind of guy who wouldn't associate with someone who befriended her brother. Because if he was, his sweet smile and gentle mannerisms would be a complete waste.

"I've known Jules since we were in Sunday school together. I wouldn't miss her wedding. But I'm worried that I won't see her after that."

"Why?" Betty asked with genuine concern.

"I'd imagine there's a good chance when she shows up at her surprise wedding she might lose her mind and run for the mountains, never to be seen again. I also feel obligated to be there in case the stress induces labor and I have to deliver the baby in your backyard."

Betty frowned, again finding herself at the receiving end of sarcasm. "Françoise will make a memorable entrance into this world, but she won't do it that day. She's a lady, with Grafton blood, and thus she'll have impeccable timing."

"Françoise huh?" Josh sat back and folded his arms. "I've already been warned about that. It's literally written in Jules's labor plans not to let you next to the birth certificate just in case."

Willow let out a snicker. "I told you. There is a reason no one throws surprise weddings."

Betty looked down at her notebook and scratched down a note. "And I've just added another song. And for you," she eyed Josh, "you're officially in charge of cleanup. You might want to bring a change of clothes, there will be loads of dishes."

"Oh man," Josh groaned as he banged his hand down on his desk lightly. "How many people are going to be there?"

"Not as many as I thought would come, but you know how people are here. Closed-minded about things they don't understand. They are very uneasy about Willow and Jedda being in town."

"Wait, why are they uneasy about me?" Willow asked, sitting forward and taking a clear interest in the conversation again.

"You're the sister of the murderer with the dangerous ex-boyfriend. And you have an incredible singing voice," Josh said matter-of-factly. "I threw in the last part. It's like a bad game of telephone, you have to add something every time you hear the rumors."

"Nice. So all these people we've been seeing all morning, who have been graciously declining, have been actually judging the hell out of me the whole time?"

"If judging were an Olympic sport, Edenville would medal every year," Josh said casually, shrugging his shoulders at the unavoidable truth.

"Great." Willow rolled her eyes and flipped her long hair off her shoulder.

"You'll get used to it," Josh promised, settling his face even further into the nice guy look.

"I don't intend to be here long enough to get used to anything."

Betty patted her leg and smiled empathetically. "I know it sucks, dear."

"Sucks?" Willow and Josh asked in unison.

"Yes, kids say that. I'm trying to be relatable. Bobby says I have to stop saying stuff like people in this town can be as mean as a skillet full of rattlesnakes over a campfire. I'm trying to say more current things, to keep up with all you kids."

After an uncomfortably long pause, Josh cleared his throat and dove into a new topic. "Willow, how is Jedda doing? Has he seen a therapist yet?"

"No, he's worried about how his mental health could be misconstrued and used against him. He hasn't had any problems since we left that day and he's trying to stay as relaxed as possible. He's been working out again. So far so good."

"That can't be easy when his sister is in danger," Josh said, his face painted with concern, but his words cutting Willow like a knife.

"I'm not in danger. I'm fine, and that has nothing to do with Jedda. I don't intend to have him fight my battles for me. I'm not a little kid chained to the wall anymore." Willow stood suddenly and unwelcomed tears filled her eyes. What had just come over her? These exact words had run through her mind for hours last night as she lay staring at the ceiling in Jules's pink childhood bedroom. But she hadn't intended to say them here. It was like having a loaded gun. She wanted the ammunition in the chamber, the words practiced and ready if she felt cornered and needed to use them, but clearly, this was not the right scenario. This was an overreaction that she didn't know if she could get out of.

"Chained to the wall?" Josh asked in a quiet and empathetic voice that made Willow feel even worse. "I'm sorry." Josh gestured for her to sit down again. "I didn't mean anything by it and I shouldn't have been so inconsiderate. I'm just worried about him. Untreated stress and anxiety can be dangerous. But it wasn't my place to imply that you were the cause. Way out of line."

Willow wasn't accustomed to apologies. She'd lived in a world of privilege for years and in that odd realm of reality very few people tended to take responsibility for where they went wrong. Most times people felt entitled and above any kind of wrongdoing on their part. This earnest exchange took her by surprise.

"She forgives you," Betty said as she stood and looped her arm with Willow's. "She doesn't look like she does, but she does."

Willow couldn't find the words, but she nodded almost imperceptibly in agreement as Betty turned them both and headed for the door.

"Don't forget those extra clothes for cleanup duty. And you better come early to help set up," Betty called over her shoulder as they headed through the office lobby and to the street.

"Well weren't those some interesting fireworks between you two," Betty said, nudging at Willow's ribs.

"I don't know what came over me. I shouldn't have said that."

"Sweetie, you can act all you like as though nothing is wrong and that you have all this figured out, but occasionally the truth is going to bubble up. It's okay. Josh is a good man. He won't hold it against you. As a matter of fact I think he likes you."

"What?" Willow asked, her cheeks flushed and hot at the thought of it.

"I just thought there was a bit of a spark there between you two. Oh, maybe I'll make him your assistant at the wedding instead. He can carry your music equipment. And don't you worry, like I said, he's a real good man. Good to his mama, kind and compassionate in every way. As long as you can overlook his profession."

"What are you talking about?" Willow asked, stopping in her tracks and tugging slightly at Betty's arm that was still looped with hers.

"I mean, he kind of stares at hoo-has all day, but it's very clinical. You shouldn't let that bother you at all."

Willow let out a little laugh, "Betty, I think Josh is probably a great guy. He's good looking and—"

A familiar voice cut in from behind them and it sent shivers down Willow's spine. "Moving on already? I thought for sure you'd be caught up on me a little longer," Brad said as he grabbed Willow's arm and in one move spun both she and Betty around to face him. “Looks like you don’t have your shotgun this time, Mrs. Clampett.”

“I don’t need a shotgun, boy. This here is downtown Edenville. The place I lived my whole life, the place my folks lived their whole life. All I need to do is let out a whistle and people would come running to string you up.”

“Word is people here think you bring trouble to their quiet little town. Are you sure they’d be so quick to come to your rescue?” he asked, raising his eyebrow, daring her to answer. He turned his attention back toward Willow. “I was hoping your brother was here. I’m dying to meet him.” He sneered and pulled Willow by her elbows into him. “I gave you a chance to turn over what you had on your laptop and you didn’t. Now I’m thinking you probably told all your little slack-jawed local yokels here what you know. Big mistake.”

“I haven’t told them anything,” Willow insisted, her head turned away and her eyes closed in anticipation of what might come.

Brad freed one of her arms and ran a finger across the soft exposed skin of her collarbone. “I forgot how nice your skin felt.” He looped his finger around the chain of the necklace that hung on her neck and yanked it, breaking the clasp and tucking it into his pocket.

“Is there a problem here?” Josh demanded, stepping out of his office door and folding his arms across his chest as he stared down Brad.

“Oh, is this the guy you have the hots for?” Brad asked, tightening his grip on Willow’s arms and brushing his lips against her ear. “He can’t do what I do to you, baby.”

“Why don’t you move along,” Josh said firmly as he took another step forward.

"And what are you going to do about it if I don't?" Brad asked, not even sparing a glance in Josh's direction.

"Are you asking if I plan to kick your ass? The answer is no; I hope I don't have to. You know why? I'm a goddamn grown-up, and this is my place of business. So I'm doing the adult thing here and telling you to move on. Let her go and keep walking."

"Fine, I'll go, but Willow is coming with me. We have some things to talk about," he said, yanking her forward.

"Like hell," Betty snapped as she grabbed a handful of Brad's hair and pulled it down until his head bent awkwardly to the side.

"Whoa," Josh said, stepping forward to separate them.

"Break it up," an officer shouted as he stepped around the corner toward them.

"R.D.," Betty said, releasing Brad's hair and pointing accusingly at him. "You get this boy's hands off her right now and you throw him in jail. Get that damn restraining order."

"No need for that, officer," Brad insisted with a devilish smile, "just a friendly chat and a hug." He pulled Willow's body into his and whispered into her ear. "You just got all these little buddies of yours in deep shit. My dad's getting involved and you know what that means. Hope you're ready for this shit." He let her go, forcefully pushing her backward into Betty's arms. "See ya," he called over his shoulder.

"Oh, I don't think so, you little piece of shit, get your ass back here right now," R.D. shouted, pointing to the spot on the sidewalk just in front of him.

"Excuse me?" Brad asked, turning back to face them and twisting his face in confused arrogance.

"Get your pretentious, pretty-boy ass back here right now before I toss you in jail. And it's a bumpy ride to the holding cell. I can almost guarantee you'd be beat to shit by the time you got there," R.D. said as he pointed again to the spot in front of him. Brad walked reluctantly toward him with his hands jammed into his pockets, looking down at his feet as R.D. continued. "You don't run this town. You're not even welcome in this town. If I ever see you put your hands on anyone, in any way, ever again, I will personally drive your ass back to New York and make sure you never have a passing thought about stepping foot in Edenville again. We have our own brand of justice down here, and if you mess with one of ours, we make sure you pay. And not even your daddy has enough money to pay that debt, trust me." R.D. was speaking down into Brad's face like a father might scold a child. Through gritted teeth and narrowed eyes, the threats were hitting their mark. "Now go on." R.D. tossed Brad backward the same way Brad had just done to Willow.

When Brad was out of sight Josh put his hand on Willow's shoulder, but she quickly shook him off. "Are you all right?" he asked, trying to get her averted eyes to connect with his, but to no avail.

"Don't look at me like that. I'm fine. I'm not some battered woman. You don't know what this is all about."

R.D. and Betty stepped aside to have their own conversation. Willow could see it consisted of an enormous amount of crazy hand gestures from Betty.

"I'd like to know, if you'd tell me," Josh said, lowering his voice slightly. "Maybe there is something I can do to help you."

"You sound like everyone else right now. As if this is just something you can swoop in and fix. Trust me, if it were that easy I'd have already taken care of it myself. You've been here your whole life, you don't understand the world I'm coming from and the power people like Brad and his father have."

"No one is completely above the law. You heard R.D., he'll arrest him if he gives you any more trouble. All I'm asking is to know more about what's going on."

"You want to know about me, watch the news. Search my name on the Internet. It's all there, every messy detail of what they've twisted into my story."

"I don't want that version. I don't want the version they tell at the diner or what some reporter on television is saying. I'm just trying to—"

"Don't. Stop trying. It's ridiculous and impossible." Willow's nerves were fried and her heart was still racing at an unimaginable speed. The hand Josh was reaching out to her didn't feel like a lifeline, it felt like just one more attempt at fixing her that wouldn't work. One more set of disappointed eyes that would be staring at her when all this was over.

"Well that's the spirit," Josh shot back, pulling open the door to his office and slipping back inside.

R.D. and Betty moved back toward her looking as though she was made of fragile glass. "Miss, I'm sorry you're having trouble. I've let all my men know to keep an eye out for Brad and make sure he's not causing you any more problems."

"Thanks," Willow said, rubbing at the sore spots on her arms.

"You should know though," R.D. started, but stopped abruptly when Betty slapped at his arm.

"I told you not to tell her."

"She needs to be aware of the situation. Miss, Brad's father called in some favors and in the process tried to send a very clear message to the police department here in Edenville. His son was not to be arrested or harmed in any way. He was throwing his weight around, mixing it up with a whole bunch of promises and threats."

"I figured it wouldn't be long until he got to you guys too," Willow said, shrugging off the news.

"A year or so ago, that would have been true but we're a new department now. We don't bend to power and we don't trade for deals. Those days are over. The law is the only thing that drives us. Now, the flip side of that coin is that his father will be looking for something to happen to him down here, and now that he's pissed at our response he'll bring all he's got down on us if his boy gets hurt in anyway."

"How would he get hurt?" Willow asked, not understanding R.D.'s warning.

"You've got a lot of people looking out for you. I doubt they'll stand by and watch Brad try to hurt you in one way or another. All it will take is one of them flying off the handle and striking out against Brad and this tinderbox will blow. The worst-case scenario is if Jedda does something. Thomas Angelo will bring down hell on this place, and Jedda won't stand a chance. I hear he's got buddies with cameras trying to catch us all stepping a toe out of line or being unlawful toward him."

"That's why he mentioned my brother," Willow said, shaking her head in disbelief. "So he wants someone to attack him? He's goading everyone on. Especially Jedda."

"We're not going to let that happen. Now that we know his game, we're not going to play," Betty assured her as she patted Willow's back tenderly.

"Nothing we can do about it right now," Willow said, stepping away from them and heading down the street.

"You're coming to the wedding right, R.D.?" Betty asked over her shoulder as she hustled to catch up with Willow.

"Yes ma'am," R.D. called, tipping the front of his hat down in her direction.

"Good boy, R.D., good boy."

Chapter Ten

Jedda kept reminding himself that Crystal could do better than him. Much, much better than him. Like a skipping record, his inner voice relentlessly repeated the chants of a reality. You'll ruin her life. She deserves more. Occasionally though, those words were drowned out by the sound of her sweet voice saying his name. Or her laugh dancing across the spring breeze.

Today they had a job to do, and Jedda liked that. He enjoyed knowing what was expected of him, and even more he enjoyed the companionship of Crystal. They'd been tasked with clearing the path that would lead to the field for the wedding. Jedda had found a handsaw and some work gloves in the shed. Crystal, her hair tied back with a purple bandana, had borrowed a pair of overalls from Jules and work boots from Betty.

They'd been out under the sun for two hours and though it wasn't a particularly hot day, they'd both worked up a sweat. Jedda had cut down all the limbs that had grown across the path while Crystal pulled them away and snipped off any small tangled vines that could trip someone up. Thorns scratched at their skin and mud matted on the knees of their pants, but judging by the smiles on their faces, a passerby might assume they were having a romantic picnic, rather than doing manual labor.

"I haven't worked like this in years," Crystal said as she wiped her gloved hand across her forehead, leaving behind a trail of dirt. "I used to love to garden with my grandmother."

"You just smudged mud all over your face," Jedda laughed, pulling off his own glove and using his hand to brush away the mess on her face. He hesitated there for a minute, letting his fingers linger before dropping his hand quickly down to his side.

"Thanks," she said quietly as she looked longingly up into his eyes. She was begging to be kissed. It was plainly written on her face. Her skin smelled like fresh flowers and every time the breeze blew, the scent would distract him and he'd have to close his eyes to refocus.

"Do you hear that?" he asked as he turned toward the house. "I think someone just pulled in. Maybe Willow and Betty are back from town."

Crystal smiled and pulled off her gloves, tucking them into the pockets of her overalls. "Let's go see."

They walked the path side by side, showing their hard work was finished. Their arms were touching slightly, just brushing occasionally as they moved. Jedda's desire to reach out and hold her hand was so powerful the only way he could avoid doing so was shoving his hands deep into his own pockets.

"That's not Betty's car," Jedda said, stopping in his tracks and taking his hand from his pocket to swing an arm up to block Crystal from taking another step. "It's Brad," Jedda whispered, tucking Crystal back into the thicker woods.

As he stepped forward he was met with her quiet protest. "Where are you going?" she asked him, clamping down on his bicep as if she were holding on for dear life.

"I'm going to see what the hell he thinks he's doing here. He's probably looking for that laptop and who knows what he'll do to the house. Not to mention, Willow and Betty could come home any minute."

"You're right," Crystal agreed, but didn't let up on his arm. "That's why we're going to go up there together and talk to him. But that's it. Do you feel like you can control yourself?"

"No," Jedda admitted, "but I'm going to try, and judging by your grip on my arm, even if I can't, I'm pretty sure you can keep me in line."

They walked slowly toward the house, Crystal just a step behind Jedda, whose arm was still protectively stretched across the front of her.

"What are you doing?" Jedda boomed as he watched Brad peer inside the windows of the front of the house.

"There you are," Brad answered with a maniacal grin. "Ah, and I can tell the note that was left for you didn't do the trick. Getting fired wasn't enough?" he asked, gesturing with his chin over at Crystal.

"You've got no business being here, Brad. You aren't welcomed," Crystal said in a solid voice as she felt Jedda's hand clench into a fist.

"I'm here to get something that's mine."

"It's not here," Crystal answered as she took a step forward. "Michael's already taken the laptop. I'm happy to give you his phone number and you can take that matter up with him"

"She gave it to the fucking lawyer?" Brad snapped as he slammed his fist into the wall of the house.

"Yes, so there is nothing here for you."

"That's where you're wrong. If they had a case against me, they'd have arrested me already. Which means I still have time to convince Willow that coming up against me is the worst thing she could do." Brad paced in a small area around the porch as he whispered angrily to himself.

"And how's that?" Jedda asked, moving toward the porch and stopping only at the soft touch of Crystal's hand on his back. "She's not afraid of you. None of us are."

"You don't understand what I can do to you. To all of you. With one phone call, I can have this house burned to the ground, and then mysteriously, you'd find out the insurance policy for it was canceled last week. And that's just the start of it. Crystal can attest to the fact that I can get people fired pretty damn quickly. I most certainly can get your ass thrown back in prison for the rest of your life, considering you shouldn't have been let out in the first place. You don't know what my father is capable of."

"Actually," Crystal said through gritted teeth, "I grew up in New York and spent years working in the legal system, so I know exactly what your father and his firm do on a regular basis. I know exactly how they bend the law to suit themselves and destroy anyone in their way. But this isn't New York. And you don't know who you're messing with here."

"No," Brad said, pulling his sunglasses off and wiping them clean on his designer T-shirt. "This is the middle of fucking-nowhere and that means I can bury all of you and no one would give a shit. Now, I'm significantly closer to the shotgun that old crackpot keeps on the fridge than either of you. I'm sure she doesn't lock the door, probably keeps the thing loaded. It wouldn't take much for me to go in there and grab it, shoot you, sweetheart, and then wait until those other two bitches get home and shoot them, too. Who do you think they'd blame for it? The likely suspect would have to be the guy who already killed a couple people. They'd clearly blame the murderer."

"That's enough," Crystal said, pushing Jedda back as he made a move for the porch. "If you're going for that gun, then go for it. Enough of the psychobabble bullshit. We're not afraid of you and neither is Willow. Whatever she has on you, it must be pretty bad, enough to take you down, because you're the only one who looks scared at the moment."

"If she'd really turned that evidence over I'd be in jail already, which means she's smart enough to know what I can do, and scared enough to know I'll do it. She also knows what will happen to her if she does bust me. Even if I'm locked up, my father and his contacts will never leave her alone. She's seen it first hand. My father is invested in this now, and he's putting his full weight behind getting this buried. No small town bullshit is going to protect her from that."

"Even if she gives you the laptop," Crystal began, shrugging her shoulders up at him, "how will she know you'll leave her alone?"

Brad slapped his hand hard to his head as though he were trying to quiet the voices screaming at him. "I just want it back. My father will make the deal, he'll be sure this is dead. That's what he does. He'll be able to look in her eyes and see that she's completely broken. That she understands we can crush her and anyone she loves, and then he'll know she won't try that shit ever again. He has a gift. He can always tell when a beaten-down dog won't bite again. You can tell when you're the master and she's given in to that. Right now, I can tell she has some fight left in her. But that won't last long. If she doesn't give me that laptop, I'll make sure she spends the rest of her life regretting it."

"You'll never touch her again," Jedda growled, the veins in his neck throbbing under his clenched tight skin.

"That's where you're wrong, killer. I can get to her anywhere, anytime. I'm going to ruin her life one person at a time. One catastrophe at a time. I can get closer to her than you can imagine." He reached into his pocket and pulled out the necklace he ripped from her neck earlier that morning. He tossed it down into Jedda's hands and laughed crazily. "She left the house in that this morning didn't she?"

Jedda inspected it and then clasped his hand tightly around it, completely ready to choke Brad to death with it. The idea of this monster being within arms reach of Willow made his blood surge through his body at a speed that made him fear he'd implode. His ears were ringing and his skin tingled; he was teetering between the wave of anxiety that had washed over him yesterday and the undertow of rage that had landed him in jail all those years ago. He wasn't sure which force would be stronger, which would drive his next move.

Brad ran his hands arrogantly through his hair as he spoke. "Anything your folks did to her when she was little is going to feel like a tropical vacation compared to what I'm going to do if she screws with me."

That was it, the tipping point that sent Jedda plunging with a headlong dive off the edge of fury. Any indecision about how he felt, what he should do was gone. Jedda charged up the stairs, shaking Crystal off his arm with such force he nearly knocked her over.

"Jedda don't," she screamed in a shrill and desperate tone. She raced up behind him, clawing and pulling on his shirt. "It's what he wants. He wants you to hurt him so he can send you back to prison. He's sick."

As Jedda's large fists clamped into rock hard weapons, a car horn blew loudly behind him. Sirens started to blare as Bobby's car pulled into the long dirt driveway. It was enough to distract Jedda from the blinding rage flowing through him and give Crystal time to wedge her body between Jedda and Brad.

Bobby's car came skidding to a halt just in front of the steps. He bolted, leaving the door swinging open. He flew up behind Jedda in a flash. "Don't touch him, Jedda," he shouted, putting his body between the two men, sending Crystal falling clumsily to the side then steadying herself on the porch railing. Jedda's mind instantly went to her. Had he hurt her? Did his blind rage cause her pain? He was already letting the guilt bite at his heart. Bobby's voice pulled him back to the moment.

"He's trying to get you to hit him. He's likely got someone here, out in the woods ready to snap some pictures or a video. He planned this."

Bobby slowly backed Jedda up, down the stairs, and to his car. "Stay," he demanded, pointing authoritatively at him.

Bobby turned his attention back to Brad, while Jedda tried to steady himself against the hood of his cruiser. "You've been warned to stay off this property, Brad. If you come out here again you will be arrested, or maybe if we're lucky you'll be shot for trespassing. I already heard about your run-in with Betty and Willow this morning. I know the game you're playing, trying to get everyone down here to act out against you and undermine the credibility of the people who plan to take you down. Making threats to try to scare them out of coming after you. You look like a cornered animal, Brad, and people down south know how to deal with rodents. If you keep this shit up, you're going to get your ass handed to you, and it will be a whole lot sooner than you think. Now go,"

Bobby said, twisting Brad's arms behind him and leading him down the stairs.

"You've got it wrong, officer. I'm not going down, but if she doesn't back off this shit you are all going to pray for death, because my father will destroy your lives so badly that you'll wish you were never born. Speaking of born, is that lawyer's baby here yet? That'll be an easy target."

Jedda watched as Bobby's face changed suddenly from firm to furious. He swept a foot in front of Brad on the way down the stairs, but held his arms in place so that when he hit the ground it was all face into dirt, with a hard thud.

Bobby leaned down as though he intended to help Brad up off the ground, presumably putting on a good show in case there really were any cameras. He was actually holding him down into the dirt for a long moment while he hissed a threat, "This will end badly for you, Brad. If you ever threaten my godchild or anyone I care about again, I will kill you. Unless your daddy has a time machine or a witch doctor, he can't save you from that." Bobby lifted Brad to his feet and dusted the dirt off the front of his shirt for him, extending the show for anyone watching. "And I'll dump your body down the deepest abandoned mine shaft on the highest mountain in this state. No one would ever find you."

Brad groaned as he yanked open his car door and fell heavily into the front seat. He sped out of the driveway, cutting the wheels so sharp they made grooves in the dirt as rocks flew up behind him.

When the car was out of sight, Bobby spun and charged Jedda. "You can't touch him. No matter what, you can't lay your hands on him. Don't you get that?"

"He's a monster. He's going to kill Willow. I'm just supposed to let that happen? Because he's rich? Because his dad is somebody?"

"No, you idiot," Bobby shouted, shoving Jedda backward. "You're supposed to trust the people who care about both you and Willow and are here to protect you. You're supposed to realize that you going back to prison doesn't help anyone, especially Willow. Michael is looking at the evidence Willow has on her computer. He's trying to determine if it's enough to build a solid case and then who he can safely take that case to. This kid is acting like this because he's terrified, and he should be. His days are numbered."

"He's right, Jedda," Crystal said, clearly trying to sound soft and supportive as she stepped down from the porch and joined the two men. "You were seconds away from doing something you couldn't take back. And if he did have cameras out here somewhere, that would have been it for you."

"Great, how many days before he's just snatching Willow and disappearing with her? How many days until he gets someone else fired, or hurts Jules or Piper? We can't just sit here and wait."

"I know how much is on the line here. You're not shedding light on anything I don't already see. But punching him and getting yourself tossed in prison is exactly what he wants. It's an angle to punishing and scaring Willow. All I'm saying is how about we don't make things any worse than they are. I need to know, when push comes to shove, can you control yourself? Are you in control here, Jedda?"

Jedda once again balled his hands into fists and let a primal growl escape his lips and then grow into a full-on yell. "No. I don't think I can. I never claimed to be healed, I never said I could come out here and just be a normal goddamn person. No matter how much you want me to be good enough for you," he said angrily, gesturing at Crystal. "You all want me to be different from the person who pulled that trigger, but maybe I'm not. Maybe I don't feel any different. I see my sister being stalked and beaten up, and I'm just supposed to keep my cool? I can't. If I could do that then maybe I wouldn't have killed my parents. You're asking me if I'm in control, and I'm saying no. No! If I see him again, if he touches her again, I will end him. I will pull every limb from his body and I will parade him down Main Street. Because I haven't changed. Is that what you need to hear?"

"Jedda," Crystal said quietly as she reached a hand out to touch his arm. He forcibly pulled away from her and stepped onto the porch. He knew it was happening again, he could feel it taking him under. The anxiety, or whatever the hell they'd called it, was taking hold of him. He couldn't breathe and lightning bolts were shooting across his head. His palms were sweating, his mouth dry, and his world was spinning around him. He leaned backward and sank into the porch swing.

"Call Josh," he mouthed to Bobby as he put his head back and gasped for air. Crystal ran up beside him and laced her fingers with his.

"Who's Josh?" she asked Bobby, looking confused.

Bobby put his phone to his ear and held it there with his shoulder as he sat down beside Jedda and checked his pulse on his wrist.

"Who is Josh?" Crystal asked again, now more demanding.

Bobby glanced up and said flatly, “The town gynecologist.”

Chapter Eleven

"I really appreciate your coming out here tonight, Josh," Willow said as she walked him out the screen door and down to his car. "Are you sure you don't want to stay for dinner?"

"No, I need to get going before my ethical judgment kicks in and I take those ten pills back from Jedda. Those won't last him very long at this rate. He's had two serious attacks in a week. They're not curative, Willow, they may not even help him if he has another panic attack. But they're the best I could do."

"I know," she said, staring down at her shoes. "You heard everything being said in there tonight, can you blame him for being afraid to see a doctor about it? You wanted to know more about what was going on, and now you do."

"I can understand his point about not wanting to see a doctor, but it doesn't make it any less necessary. He's in a tailspin right now and I can tell it's a very fine line for him between anxiety and violence."

Willow shrugged her shoulder helplessly. "I am really sorry for the way I spoke to you earlier today, Josh."

"Which time?" he asked, raising his eyebrows at her as though he wanted her to know how much of a jerk she'd been.

"Pretty much everything I've said to you before this conversation. I'm sorry. You seem like a great guy and I didn't treat you very nicely. I have a lot going on. It's what makes this request so hard for me." Willow tucked her hair behind her ears and bit at her lip. "I don't like asking people for help, but I know I have to. If I don't,

Jedda won't get any better. I'm just not sure I should," Willow said, looking torn.

"It's now or never because I'm heading out," Josh said, pulling his keys from his pocket.

"I need a ride," Willow said in a hushed voice. "I've made the decision that the best thing for everyone is for me to go. But I need you to take me to the bus station or train station or something. And I don't mean the closest one. I want to go a few towns over, at least."

"Are you afraid Brad will find you at the closest one?"

"Yes, but I'm also afraid they will find me," Willow continued with a glance back at the house.

"That should tell you something," Josh said, looking earnestly into her eyes.

"It does. It tells me that they are really good people who would do anything, and I mean anything, for me, and they deserve better than what they are about to get. The best thing I can do is go."

"You're just going to walk right by them with your things and think they won't stop you? If that's the case you're underestimating them greatly. All together like that, they'll find a way to convince you."

"My bag's already in your car," Willow said, handing him the one key missing from the set he was holding.

"That's impressive," Josh said, looking down at the set and then back at Willow. "These were in my pants pocket."

"Don't ask me to show you how I got them. I won't do it twice," Willow grinned, hoping that a flash of her smile would persuade him. She needed to run, she needed to give these people back their safety and give Jedda a real chance at freedom.

"I care about everyone in there. I don't intend to get between you and them. And, frankly, they scare me," Josh said.

"If you really do care about them, then save their lives and give me a ride. Please, Josh." Willow swallowed back her emotions, batting her wet lashes at him.

"Get in the car," Josh whispered as he clearly fought his better judgment for the second time today.

The ride was mostly silent as they weaved away from Edenville. Willow's one-word answers to general questions set the tone for the awkwardness. She knew Josh was dying to talk, maybe talk her out of leaving, but he was too nice to put her through that, and she was grateful.

"Thanks for this," Willow said again as she read the highway sign for the train station a couple miles away. She could chat for the last couple minutes of the drive, no harm in that really. The end was in sight.

"I'm not sure what it is about you that makes me act against all the sense God gave me. I'm normally the voice of reason for everyone. I don't treat people who aren't my patients. I don't nearly get in fistfights in front of my office. And I don't aid and abet a runaway. You're bringing out the worst in me," Josh said, turning the radio off as he spoke.

"That might be my superpower," Willow said, biting nervously at her nails. "I have the ability to take perfectly good people and turn their lives upside down. I'm like an emotional plague."

"I'm sure that isn't true. You're too hard on yourself."

"Let's see, Jedda was adopted by an incredible family. He had a new brother. He had a real shot at having a good life. Then he came back for me and we know how that worked out. My adoptive parents were wealthy, successful people with a great circle of friends. Now my name is flashing all over the news up there and I'm sure they're getting the same reaction I got from everyone who claimed to be my friend. I'm sure, even if they'd managed to stave off the regret of adopting me while I put them through hell growing up, it's officially sunk in for them now. And that just leaves all of you. You're an idyllic little town with picket fences where everyone knows their neighbor. I go and bring a snake down here who's hell-bent on destroying anything he thinks I'm associated with. You really want to make an argument against all that?" Willow asked, a part of her hoping maybe he would have something to say. Maybe he'd hold an answer she'd been desperate to hear for years.

"You're right," Josh said, nodding his head. "They should start working on a vaccine to protect people from you. I'm going to call the CDC after I drop you off."

"Nice." Willow rolled her eyes and went back to nervously biting her nails.

"You aren't an emotional plague," he said, patting her leg gently. "You've had some tough times and those don't just evaporate overnight. You've got to fight your way out of them. And it seems like you're trying."

"Collateral damage isn't something I can live with. Not more of it anyway. Leaving is my best option. Or it's at least best for everyone else. They might not know it right now, but deep down inside I'm sure they want me to go."

"I don't." Josh shrugged, leaving his hand lingering on her leg for one more moment. "If it's worth anything, I think you should stay."

"Why?" Willow asked, again grudgingly wanting Josh to say something that might actually reach her fortified heart.

"I've lived here my whole life. Up until last year, not much ever happened. I took over my father's practice and seemed to just step right onto the path he'd cleared for me. I feel like my life is pretty much already set up for me. And I realized it isn't even what I wanted for myself, for a career. You're the only thing that's happened lately that makes me feel like maybe my life won't be boring and predetermined. I know once you leave things will go right back to the way they've always been. You're like a breath of fresh air, and I've been suffocating. You might be exactly what I need." Willow was staring out the window, pulling the zipper of her coat. She was sure Josh was waiting for her to speak but she couldn't. There was no answer inside her, no matter how hard she searched.

"Plus," Josh said, taking the weight out of the moment. "Betty is going to string me up when they realize I drove you out here. Bobby and Michael will kick my ass. And Jules, for the love of God, I don't know what Jules will do to me."

"I suggest you wear a cup. I've seen her in action." Willow smirked as she slipped her coat back on and pulled her bag onto her lap. "You can just drop me by the door if you don't mind."

"I do mind," Josh said, navigating away from the front entrance and toward the parking lot. "I'm making sure you get on that train safely. There's no way in hell I'm just leaving you here, not knowing you made it out all right. Non-negotiable, so save your breath."

"Fine," Willow said with a roll of her eyes.

The train station was relatively deserted this Friday night and Willow was grateful for the quiet corner she and Josh found to wait in. She hated the hustle and bustle that came with school in New York and dreaded the idea of public transportation, but this was her best way out. Growing up on a small island whose only connection to the mainland was an old, slow ferry made her feel isolated in the best way possible. She never felt trapped there as many of her classmates did. She felt safe, like the island was a cocoon. Leaving it had been difficult, and maybe that's why she'd found herself caught up so quickly in Brad.

After twenty more minutes of nail-bitingly awkward silence, Willow felt someone slide in next to her on the bench she and Josh were perched on. "Excuse me?" Willow groaned as the person thudded against her body.

"You're going to need a good excuse," Piper said, raising her eyebrows accusingly at both of them.

"Shit," Josh cursed as he shot to his feet to try to explain. "She forced me. At knife point."

"Save it, Josh," Piper said, quieting him with the wave of her hand. "I don't care why you drove her, I'm interested in why she left."

"I'll leave you two alone," Josh said, clumsily stepping away from them, but Piper pulled him back with a tug of his sleeve.

"Nope, if you're a good enough friend to be the getaway car then you can hear all this." Piper pointed down at the bench and he sat back down dutifully.

"Piper, how did you find me?" Willow asked with an air of defeat.

"I've run away quite a bit myself. I know enough to pop the battery out of my cell phone so my cop friends can't track where I am."

"I did," Willow said angrily pulling her disassembled phone from her pocket.

"But he didn't. If you're going to have company they need to follow the same runaway rules, too. Now tell me why you left."

"You don't get it," Willow huffed, jamming her phone into her pocket and flopping hard against the wooden back of the bench.

"That's where you're wrong. It's why I'm here, and not any of the other people at the house who thought they should come. I'm the one person you can't pull that line with. I grew up in a hell just like yours. I know what it's like to be punished in the most hateful ways by people who are supposed to love you. I know what it's like to be so hungry you start to see things. I've been there."

"Stop. I'm not that person. I left all that and I got a second chance. I grew up on the dunes of a beautiful island with unbelievably wonderful people for parents. I went to a great school. I had everything I ever needed. I'm not that girl you're talking about. She doesn't exist."

"Fine, I don't believe you, but if that's the card you want to play I won't argue it with you. But you're mixed up about one thing. Do you think that Jedda going back to prison while protecting you would destroy him? Crush him?"

"Yes," she answered, as though it were the most obvious thing in the world. "Of course it would."

"No," Piper said, softening her voice. "Not knowing where you are, whether or not you're safe, the idea of you facing all this alone—that is what will crush him. Leaving him now would be the worst thing you could do to him."

Willow thought she'd built a pretty effective fence around her heart, but Piper's rationale was starting to put cracks in her own logic. What if she was right; what if, in his fragile state, leaving Jedda would push him over the edge? She hadn't considered that. Which is exactly why she'd wanted to leave before they could talk to her. She didn't want to think about the alternative, she didn't want to be convinced, but she was faltering now. "You really think it will crush him if I leave him now?"

Piper nodded her head vehemently. "Yes. I just saw him at the house when we realized you'd left. I know it would be too much for him. Please don't desert him now. He needs you more than you realize."

"Part of me thinks I'm the worst thing for him. I'm like a trigger, I bring him back to that terrible choice he made. And I'm putting him in the position to have to do it again."

"I think you two might need to talk, because I've never heard Jedda refer to what he did as a terrible choice. I don't think he regrets it at all. I'm not saying you can't leave, I'm just saying don't leave him like this, without a word. Give it a little more time. Give Michael a chance to work on it."

"Well, whether he says it or not, it was a mistake. One that changed both our lives."

"Yours for the better, Willow. Look at what you have now. Look at what you got for a second chance.

He'd do it all over again. He wouldn't change anything. I really believe that."

Willow looked through Piper, her gaze vacant as she realized the disconnect in this conversation. It struck her how deep the cavern of misunderstanding between her and the rest of the world was. Everyone looked at her like the lucky one. As though knowing Jedda would give his life for her again should be comforting. How wrong they were.

"That's what I'm afraid of. That he'll do it all over again. That he wouldn't hesitate," Willow whispered, talking more to herself as she stood and slipped her bag over her shoulder. "Is everyone pissed?" She looked defeated as she surrendered.

"Not at you. They understand this isn't easy," Piper answered, standing and pulling her car keys from her pocket. "Now, Josh, on the other hand, might want to take that train ticket you bought and think about starting a practice somewhere else."

"Knifepoint," Josh reiterated, putting his hands up in the air like a helpless victim. "She took me captive at knifepoint and I had no choice."

"Well you've got an hour ride back to get your stories straight. I suggest you make it airtight. I imagine there will be some kind of inquest or tribunal."

"Wait, I'm not riding back with you?" Willow asked, imploring Piper with her eyes to make this situation marginally less uncomfortable.

"No, you guys made your bed now you can lie in it," Piper said, heading toward the exit then seeming to realize what she'd just said. "Don't go lying in any actual beds for God's sake. It's a figure of speech. No need to make this thing any messier than it is. Just come right back to the house. No beds."

Willow's cheeks burned red for so many reasons right now she couldn't sort them out. Was she more embarrassed that Piper brought up the horrors of her past? That Josh had heard her secret pain spoken out loud? Or was it Piper's implication that they could end up in bed together? Any way she considered it made her think she might be sick any second if they stood there much longer.

"You're ruining my life," Josh said, tucking his hands into his pockets and shuffling his feet toward the door.

"Sorry." Willow hung her head and kept a slow pace as to not have to walk right next to him on their way back to the car.

"It's okay," Josh said, stopping and turning to face her so she'd have to catch up. "I told you I wasn't crazy about my life anyway. It could use some ruining. Not this much, but beggars can't be choosers I guess."

"I'll try to take the heat off you when we get back to Betty's. I won't let them come down too hard on you," Willow promised, finally catching up with Josh, who held the door open for her as they stepped back into the night air.

"Knifepoint, Willow. I'm not joking. Tell them you kidnapped me. It might be my only hope. Knifepoint."

Chapter Twelve

The ride back wasn't full of deep conversation about her feelings as Willow feared it might be. Josh was polite, and luckily that meant he wasn't going to try to exploit what he had heard at the train station. She had no doubt if she sat beside him and bared her soul he'd listen attentively with compassion and sympathy, but she wasn't interested in that. Mostly because she wouldn't know where to begin. How do you articulate things that almost tear you in two on a regular basis? How do you expose the conflict raging a war inside of you without sounding like a mental patient? Willow didn't have those answers, so she chose silence.

It did beg the question though: could one person really be as conflicted as she was and not be considered insane? She bounced so frequently between opposing emotions that she thought she must have some kind of personality disorder. There were moments when she found herself eternally grateful for the choice Jedda made the day he killed their parents. How lucky she was to have a second chance in this world—to go from the gutter to a life of privilege. It was the building blocks of a fairy tale. But then when her admiration for her brother's sacrifice would grow, she would start to feel like a monster, as though she were a murderer herself. How could any human being, regardless of the circumstances, condone, applaud even, the taking of someone else's life? That wasn't how the civilized world worked.

The only thing that weighed heavier on her than the burden of torn feelings about the murders themselves, was the knowledge that her brother traded his life for hers. It didn't matter that their parents were horrible people. Their murder, deserved or not, happened because of her. That means her life, the one she was handed out of the ashes of her burned down childhood, needed to be good. She had to spend her time being her best self and appreciating every minute of her second chance. She had to be eternally grateful for his sacrifice. But, frankly, there were some days mustering that happiness just wasn't possible. Some days she found herself getting sucked into the despair of knowing what her life might have been if Jedda hadn't intervened. Those thoughts would grow muddy and far away as the thoughts of what his life would have been like if he'd let her rot there or be sold off.

Who deserved it more, Willow or Jedda, and why did it seem like only one of them could have it? Why was she spared and not him? Why was she given this better life and he sentenced to solitude and punishment? She should be happy, wildly happy, and in a constant state of feeling blessed. But instead all she felt was a knot of conflicted ideas that on any given day drove her to the brink of madness. What if? Why not? Why Me?

"Seriously, Willow. They're going to be furious with me," Josh worried aloud as they approached the road leading to Betty's. He was tapping nervously on the steering wheel and shaking his leg with an antsy franticness that was wearing on Willow's frayed nerves.

"I won't let them take it out on you," she assured him. "You don't deserve it. You were just trying to help me. You're very kind."

"It seems that's what they're trying to do, too," Josh said, attempting ineffectively to make a point Willow wasn't interested in hearing right now.

"Don't waste your breath. You really wouldn't understand any of this. I barely get it myself. I'm an hour out from deciding to stay, and I already feel like I made the wrong choice. It's why I didn't want to hear from any of them. I knew they'd make some case, I'd waiver, and come back. Inevitably regretting it, which I already do."

"You got mixed up in something. Brad's a jackass trying to torment you. That's not on you. You can't feel guilty about that and you can't think no one cares about you."

"I'm going to make sure everyone knows you had no choice in taking me to the train station. Can we just leave it at that? I'm not interested in anything else."

"I don't get why it's so hard for you to take help from people. To accept a little kindness."

Willow sighed, weary of trying to explain herself. "It's wasted on me. Trust me. The last thing I want or need is people sacrificing anything for my sake. It sounds good in theory. But if you've ever been on the receiving end of it, you'd understand."

"So then what do you need? If not help, then what?"

Willow opened her mouth to speak but then promptly closed it when she realized she had no answer. No one had ever asked her that. After she was adopted, they'd told her she needed therapy, so she went. And for their sake she pretended to feel better. They'd told her she needed three tutors to catch up in school, so she worked tirelessly to learn, spent sleepless nights attempting to be what they needed. To make her brother's sacrifice seem worth it. They'd showed her how to blend in, how to carry herself, how to be this new kind of Willow, so she did as they said. No one had asked her what she needed, so now, faced with the simple question, she had no answer. She just shook her head, her eyebrows raised in surprise at this epiphany.

Their headlights cut their way down Betty's driveway and shone on all the cars still parked there. People ready to kill Josh and embrace Willow. Two things she really didn't want to happen.

Josh reached over and covered her hand with his. Putting the car in park he turned to face her, locking eyes with her in a stare she couldn't break. "Well, I guess you know what you need to do. Figure out the answer to that question and you'll have a place to start. Decide what you need, and you might be surprised who's willing to help you get it."

She thought he might lean in, and press his perfect lips against hers. Maybe he would sweep her hair out of her face and cup her cheek as his tongue explored her mouth. Any other man she'd known in this type of situation would be kissing her right now. When she found herself staring, wondering what was keeping his face way over there, she remembered. He was kind. Together. Grown up. He didn't act on impulse or desire, he acted thoughtfully and with ample regard for others' needs. She, on the other hand, didn't. She was impulsive and confused. Occasionally reckless and frequently wrong. It's how she found herself with a guy like Brad. It's why she stayed after she found out what he'd done, the crimes he'd committed. It's what made her lean in right now, and press her lips to Josh's even when she had no intention of giving him what he deserved or was hoping for. She wasn't the type of person he needed, even if he joked about excitement and drama. His life was good and steady and she was selfishly taking from him what she could. A moment of comfort, a feeling of pleasure, that she had no means of growing into anything else. She was why a good guy finished last, because in a moment of her own weakness she exploited his heart.

As his hand moved up to her cheek, their kiss growing more passionate, Willow pulled away. It was an art, keeping herself unavailable. It required incredible willpower and perfect timing. He sat there for a moment staring at her as though that kiss had changed something, as though it was the start of something, and the guilt of reality hit her. She shouldn't have kissed him.

"Willow," he said, catching her arm before she could step out of the open car door. "I won't hold you to that kiss. I won't make it something it wasn't. But next time, if you kiss me, it needs to mean something. To both of us."

There he was astounding her again. How could he see that written so clearly on her face? Another man would have taken that moment and spun it into something it wasn't. But not Josh. It's like he could read her mind or peek inside her soul. A frightening possibility.

"Okay," was all she could muster as he let her go and she stepped out of the car. They strode to the screen door and took a deep breath before they entered. Piper had beaten them back here and had clearly already briefed everyone on what had transpired. The room was full of people with scowls on their faces and arms crossed. The most intimidating of all was Betty, standing by the table holding a rolling pin in one hand and slapping the other end down into her palm. Clay rested his hand on her shoulder as though he were holding the leash of a tiger, a fruitless effort, but his job all the same.

"Josh had nothing to do with this. I didn't give him a choice," Willow said preemptively. "I think he should just head home for the night and we can see him at the wedding on Sunday."

"You think I'll let him off the hook that easy?" Betty asked, stepping forward, nose-to-nose with Josh. "You know better than this, Josh. You saw that boy in front of your office today. How could you send her into the world alone? Reckless."

Willow snickered slightly at that thought. It was likely the only time in his life Josh had been accused of that. And it was her doing. She knew the best thing Josh could do was take his lumps and ride out the anger flowing through the room. Even Willow, who didn't know these people that long, knew that much. But the spark in Josh's eyes let Willow know he wasn't going to take that route.

"She's a grown-up. At some point she needs to make the decision she thinks is best for herself."

"Really?" Bobby asked, shock spreading across his face. "You think she'd do better out there on her own? Running away is the answer?"

"No, that isn't what I'm saying. But you're all acting like she's some child who needs rescuing. I get that the situation is volatile, there is risk here, but she's an adult. And as far as I've seen, a pretty smart one. I don't think you should discount what she wants for herself and why she wants it. I think you're all overlooking something."

Jedda's tone was laced with skepticism and frustration as he spoke, "And what's that?"

"I have no idea, because, honestly, I don't know her that well, but it seems maybe none of you do either. So before you tell her what she's doing is so wrong and her plan for herself isn't the right one, maybe you should understand her better. Do a little more listening and little less demanding." Josh turned, patted Willow on the shoulder and headed for the door. She hadn't seen that coming, and judging by the saucer-sized eyes of everyone in the room, neither did they.

A few moments after he stepped out, stunned silence filling the room, Michael and Jules walked in. They glanced from one silent face to another, and finally Michael spoke. "What did I miss?"

"Willow took off, had Josh drive her to the train station in Ilksville. Piper went after her and talked her into coming home," Betty recapped, dropping her rolling pin to the table loudly.

"Willow?" Michael asked, looking at her full of confusion. "I told you I was working on things. The wheels are in motion. Why would you go now?"

"Brad grabbed me in the street today while I was out with Betty. Then came here and Jedda was seconds away from losing it on him. If Bobby hadn't pulled up he would have assaulted him, and that was Brad's plan. Maybe he had someone videoing it or something. He's trying to trap Jedda into going back to prison. He threatened your fiancée and your unborn child." She gestured over to Jules. "Sorry, but I didn't want to sit around and wait for all that to happen." Willow slipped her bag off her shoulder and shimmied out of her sweatshirt.

Michael was speechless. His lips parted to speak but nothing came out. Probably shaken by the idea of the most precious people in his life being at risk. "We knew he was going to make threats, and now that we know he's goading Jedda, we can be proactive about making sure that doesn't happen."

"You look more like you're trying to convince yourself," Willow said, taking a seat next to Jedda. "Are you positive Jedda can control himself in that situation? Can you keep Jules and your daughter safe while you try to make a case here? Because if you're the one pushing this case forward, you're one of the biggest targets and then so are they."

Jedda, looked down at his sister as though he were looking at a stranger, and Willow wanted to tell him she was. "Why are you fighting this so hard, Willow? Why are you looking for all the reasons this won't work?"

"Excuse me for being realistic," she huffed.

Michael cleared his throat and leaned himself against the wall of Betty's kitchen. "We have one other plan here." His voice cracked slightly. "I can talk to his father. Call a truce. Turn over whatever evidence I have on him and assure him we won't pursue it."

Piper locked eyes with him and spoke firmly. "None of us has asked up until this point, Michael, but now I feel like we need to hear it. What did he do? What's the crime he'd be getting away with?"

"No," Willow insisted, "we're not going to play jury here and decide if it's bad enough to risk everything. Michael knows, and you should just trust him. If he's willing to make this move then it's the right one."

The room was silent again, the ticking clock on the wall the only noise. Every eye focused on Michael's furrowed brow and clenched jaw. "We owe it to the people he hurt to get justice for his part in the crimes committed. I'm just worried that a lot more people might get hurt in the process. I've done a lot of digging around on Brad and his father. Willow is right. Their reach is far, their connections deep. Their family is talked about like a faction of the mafia rather than a law firm. I don't know if now is the best time to go up against them. Jedda being so fresh out of prison. I'm about to be a father. I think we should make a deal."

Piper made a derisive sound and looked at her friend incredulously. "That doesn't sound like the Michael I know."

"No, it doesn't, because the Michael you've always known never had so much to lose. I can't just make these decisions for myself. I have to think about my family."

"What about your contact at the FBI? Agent Stanley?" Betty asked, stepping between Piper and Michael, breaking the tension that was growing between them.

"The case isn't federal. There wouldn't be anything he could do." Michael pulled Jules into his arms.

Jules looked up into his face as she spoke. "You know we'll be fine, you need to do what you think is right. We've got lots of people here to protect us."

"This really is different, Jules. For a lot of reasons." He rubbed her stomach affectionately. "Look how close you came today to getting put back in prison, Jedda. You're having these attacks, and you're not getting treated. At some point, something is going to snap. Can you really look me in the eye and tell me if Brad were here right now, you could walk away. You could leave that alone?"

"It's easy for me to tell you right now that I could, but in the moment, something like today when he was talking about what he'd do to her, it was like I couldn't control myself. I felt like an animal. I shoved Crystal aside, I could have hurt her." Willow watched as Crystal rubbed Jedda's back gently. She felt a stabbing pain in her heart at what her problems were doing to her brother, but it was dulled slightly by the fact that he wasn't alone.

"You're doing your best, Jedda. And I'm not hurt," Crystal whispered as she smiled that full-face smile Willow constantly saw on her.

"We don't need to decide this tonight. Let's all take the weekend. It's not my decision alone to make. Really it's up to Willow to decide," he said, kissing the top of Jules's head. "Crystal, can I talk to you for a second?" He gestured for her to come out to the front yard with a forced casual look on his face.

"Sure," she shrugged, swallowing hard as though she'd just been called into the principal's office. Everyone in the house tried to busy themselves with idle conversation, but Jedda burned to know what Michael might want with Crystal. He leaned back to get a better view of them through the window. Was it about her job? Some other trouble Brad was going to cause her? He assumed Michael didn't want to burden him with any more stress, but he refused to be left out on what might be going on.

He watched as Crystal's gestures became defensive and Michael's more aggressive. They were arguing, a genuine disagreement that he couldn't begin to figure out the reason for. Suddenly Betty stood in front of him, intentionally blocking his view. "You want another glass of sweet tea?" she asked, pouring it before he even answered.

As Crystal quietly stepped back into the house Michael stayed in the doorway and gestured for Jules to come out with him. "Night," he called, a bite of anger still present on his tongue.

"We should get going, too," Bobby said, pulling Piper to her feet.

"Is the wedding still going to happen Sunday?" Clay asked in a hushed voice, as he carried an armful of dishes over to the sink.

"Yes," Betty assured definitively. "The wedding is happening. We don't let threats or bullies keep us from living our life. Those two deserve to be wed. We've got everything lined up. We're not backing down now."

"Fair enough," Bobby said wearily, kissing Betty's cheek and heading with Piper for the door. "We'll be by in the morning to help finish everything. Everyone try to stay out of trouble until then."

"Clay and I are off to bed, too. We need a good night's sleep if we're going to get all this cooking done tomorrow and be ready for the wedding the day after that," Betty said, leaving Crystal, Jedda and Willow in the kitchen.

"I'm going to head back to my hotel." Crystal slipped on her coat and grabbed her purse from the counter. "Good night." She leaned into Jedda self-consciously for a hug. She let him go quickly and hustled out the door, her cheeks blushed.

"What was that all about?" Jedda asked gesturing back outside where she and Michael had been talking.

"Nothing. Just—nothing. I'll be by tomorrow to get things ready," she said in a rushed voice as she disappeared outside.

"Is she your girlfriend or something?" Willow asked, shifting away from Jedda into a chair across from him instead.

"No. She's just a friend. But a good friend. I wonder what she and Michael were talking about."

"You don't think it's weird that she just strikes up a friendship with you out of the blue? Then comes all the way down here to 'help' you out." Willow made air quotes and a face that showed her cynicism.

"Do you have any friends?" Jedda shot back defensively.

"I did," Willow admitted as she picked at her flaking red nail polish. "Or I guess they weren't really my friends. They all kind of scattered once I was on the news. They were more Brad's friends."

"That was at school, what about before that? On the island. You must have had friends. You grew up there."

"Sorry if you expected me to be a social butterfly or something. But I wasn't. I never really connected with too many people there. I had a social circle, everyone does when you live in that kind of world. But I wouldn't call any of them friends."

"But your parents, the people who adopted you, they were good people, right?" The hopefulness in Jedda's eyes only fed the pain in Willow's heart.

"Yes. They're perfect, actually. Smart, kind, selfless. They've given me everything. I've wanted for nothing," Willow said pensively, her gloomy face not matching the happy message she was portraying.

Jedda didn't seem to understand what was bothering her. He couldn't seem to grasp the disconnect between what Willow's life turned into versus how she felt.

"I'm happy that things worked out for you. I know this is a bump in the road, but it will get better. And you can go back to how things were before. Whatever you and Michael decide, I'll support it. If you want to face this guy head on, I'll be there. If you want to make a deal, I'll support you on that, too. It's hard for me to not react the way I do when you're in trouble, but I'm trying."

"You'd do anything for me. You've made that very clear," Willow groaned with an air of exhaustion.

"You say that like it's a bad thing. I've got your back."

"It's not a bad thing. It's just not quite as comforting as you would think, knowing someone would give up everything for you."

"I don't know what you mean." Jedda's face was twisted with pain as he reached across and held her hand.

"I don't either," Willow said, sweeping away the hair that had fallen in front of her face. "I'm going up to bed. I'll see you in the morning."

"I hope so. Don't run, Willow. I wouldn't be able to take it if you left now. You get that, right?"

"Yeah." Willow headed toward the stairs. "I won't leave again." She felt a vise twist over her chest as she said the words. The idea of being trapped made her feel like an animal being hunted. She knew already as she pulled herself up the stairs that she wouldn't sleep. She braced for another long night staring at the ceiling and fighting with herself about what she hated more. Did she hate what Jedda had done, or did she hate herself for the gratitude it made her feel? Did she hate the pressure that came from being given a second chance, or hate herself for not appreciating it and living it to the fullest? Her mind was a twisted knot of conflict as she flopped down onto the pink, frilly bedspread and buried her face in the fluffy pillow.

The tears came like a faucet had been spun open. She should have gotten on the train. She should have left and not looked back. Jedda would have been surrounded by all these people to support him, and she'd be free of the burden that came from protection she didn't deserve and sacrifice she was tired of people making in her name. She shouldn't have kissed Josh. Not only because she wasn't good for him, but because it made her feel something she wished it hadn't. It made her want him. More than just physically. She yearned for his kind words and logical calmness.

Her eyes burned with the salt of her tears as she rolled and stared at the clock. Let the count down until morning begin. This pain would be with her until the sun rose and the day could distract her from her self-hate. Nine hours. She'd need to fend herself off for that long.

Chapter Thirteen

They'd all spent the morning finishing the final preparation for Sunday's wedding and now it was time to relax, or so they hoped.

"I think I've got it now," Crystal said as she stepped out onto the porch in Jules's wedding dress. It was a simple silk gown, strapless with delicately subtle beading on the bodice. Everyone turned her way and broke into silly laughter as they saw the beach ball she'd tucked underneath the middle of it to try to size the dress correctly. "All I needed was a prop." She laughed as she patted the ball.

Jedda was the first to stop laughing, his mind getting distracted by the sight of this beautiful girl. Though just pretending, she was a very convincing bride, and mother-to-be, for that matter.

It added a layer of worry to his mind. He'd pretty much written off the idea of ever being a parent. Wouldn't she want that for herself? He wasn't even convinced he'd changed enough to be a functioning, non-violent member of society, let alone a husband or father. Could he really ever be enough to fulfill what she envisioned for her life?

Clearly reading the seriousness that had come over Jedda's face, Betty sidled up to him and nudged his ribs. "She ain't pregnant, boy, it's a beach ball. Get a hold of yourself. Don't go letting the fear of the future steal the fun of the present. You can only live for today."

"I, um . . . I wasn't, I was just . . ." Jedda mumbled, embarrassed to be so easily read.

"Just let things happen how they may. Don't overthink it. I find the brain to be a real son of a bitch. It's the heart that seems to know the way. So follow it."

Crystal turned and headed back in the house to hang the dress and was back in a flash to sit by Jedda.

"It's kind of like assigned seating out here, isn't it?" Jedda asked as he sank onto his chair on the porch.

Bobby and Piper leaned against each other as they moved the swing back and forth rhythmically.

"It's just how it happened," Bobby answered as he laced his fingers through Piper's. "This is really where we fell in love. We spent a lot of time out here and no matter what we were dealing with, this place felt safe."

Piper's eyes lit as she nuzzled into Bobby's arms. "I don't ever think it's a good idea to compare troubles, Jedda. Everyone's journey is his or her own. I'm learning a lot about that in school right now. So I won't sit here and tell you that I know what you're going through or that I know how you should deal with it. But for me, I found a place that I could come back to when I was feeling out of control. When I was ready to run, I held onto the chains of this swing and reminded myself that I deserved to be happy. I think it's important to have something to hold onto." Whether she was meaning to or not, her statement felt like an implication for Jedda to grab hold either physically or figuratively to Crystal, and that pressure showed on Jedda's face.

When he didn't respond Crystal cleared her throat and tried to make the situation more comfortable. "Piper what are you going to school for?"

"I'm going to start with social work and child advocacy. That's really the next step in my own journey. I bottled up a lot of my past and felt like I had no one to turn to. I think it will be important for me to make sure other kids don't feel the same way. It helps me on the hard days."

"You still have hard days?" Jedda asked, looking up from his shoes.

"Sure." Piper nodded. "I wonder why it had to be me and not some other kid. I struggle with bad memories and even some guilt. But on those days, it's nice to settle back onto this swing and remember I'm not in that life anymore."

"Porch swing love," Bobby said, leaning in and kissing Piper, who couldn't contain her smile even through the kiss.

"What is this, a high school make-out party?" Betty asked as she stepped back on to the porch with Clay on her arm.

"Oh, I hope so," Clay said, spinning Betty around and kissing her as she pretended to fight him off.

"We were just going back to work," Bobby said as he hopped to his feet and Piper followed closely behind. "We've got to finish the last part of the arbor and then we're done."

"We have to sweep the porch and wipe down the windows and then we're done too," Crystal said, as she stood and reached for the broom.

"I'll finish the porch," Betty said. "You two have been working hard all morning. Why don't you go for a walk or something?"

"Where's Willow?" Jedda asked, trying to see into the house over Betty's shoulder. "She hasn't come outside all day."

"She's upstairs, likely working on music for the wedding." Betty took the broom and shooed them away as if they were pesky animals.

Jedda and Crystal headed down the driveway to the street. "Where are we supposed to walk?" she asked as she tucked her hands into the pockets of her sweater.

"I don't know," Jedda said, absent-mindedly kicking at a stone. "I don't really feel like walking anyway."

"What's on your mind?" she asked, tilting her head up in empathy at him. "You can talk to me about it. Having some memories of your childhood, remembering something about your parents?"

"I wish you wouldn't do that."

"Do what?"

"Smile the way you do. Offer to listen to me. Smell so good. I just wish you wouldn't."

"I can skip a shower tomorrow morning if that helps."

"Great, I'll add sense of humor to the list, too." Jedda groaned.

"What list is that?" she asked, and Jedda could tell she was fighting to not be insulted.

"The list of things that make you perfect and make it hard for me to remember why I shouldn't kiss you. I don't want this, Crystal," Jedda said, gesturing back and forth between them with his hands. "I don't want us. All I want is for my sister to be okay, and this is distracting me from that. It's the same thing that happened when we were kids. I took my eyes off her, and I almost lost her forever because of it."

"I'm not trying to distract you," Crystal said, the smile fleeing from her face, something that rarely happened. "You act as though I'm throwing myself at you."

"I know you're not." Jedda leaned up against the old stone wall that lined the driveway. "I just hear Piper talking about how Bobby helped her through her stuff and I feel like everyone is just waiting for something to happen between you and me. Like you're just waiting."

"I told you I wasn't."

"I know what you said, but I look at you and it's an actual battle not to give in to it, to the desire to hold you and kiss your lips. I can't lose focus on Willow again. I can't get distracted."

"I understand that she's your sister and that you love her but at some point you need to start seeing that your life is worth something also. You weren't put on this planet solely to protect her. You deserve some happiness too."

"I can't be happy if she isn't safe. If you can't understand then there really is nothing here for us." Jedda stared at the branches of an oak tree.

"I'm not saying you should throw her to the wolves, and I'm not saying you should run away with me and we should live happily ever after. You're twisting things around. Seeing you out here yesterday with Brad, watching what you were on the verge of doing was frightening and I just want to know you're not going to jeopardize your future."

"I can't make that promise. I don't know what will happen."

"You're saying it as if you don't get any say in it. These are your choices to make. You can't go acting as though you have no say in how you act. You're standing on the edge of the same decision you had to make all those years ago, and I want to believe you'd handle it differently. Judging by yesterday, that's not the case."

"I warned you that you'd be let down. I tried to tell you the odds weren't in your favor," Jedda reminded her as he stood and turned his back on her.

"You're talking about this like it's some self-fulfilling prophecy. Like you've already decided to take care of Brad yourself."

"I have," Jedda said, shrugging and heading back to the house. "If he comes near her again, that'll be it for him."

"So that's it. Nothing else matters to you? You don't care about your own life? You don't care enough about anyone else?" Even without turning around, Jedda could tell Crystal's eyes were wet with tears, her words catching in her throat.

"You should go back to New York," he said as he headed for the house. "There's no point putting yourself through this."

"That's the difference between you and me. I don't give up on anyone I care about. I'm not leaving here until I'm damn well ready," Crystal said, picking up her pace and passing Jedda on the way back to the house. "You can find a different way. I believe in you."

Jedda stopped in his tracks as he watched Crystal stomp up the steps to the porch and act as though nothing had happened. She picked up a rag and started helping Betty. He'd just shot a cannon straight across her bow. He'd told her to go. A lesser woman would have grabbed her bag, hopped in her car, and angrily left, putting him and Edenville in her rearview mirror. But not Crystal. She was the kind of person who loved who he might be, rather than who he was. He wasn't sure if that made him the luckiest man in the world or if it made her the owner of the most defenseless heart he'd ever met. Either way a warmth of relief spread across his chest as he realized she wasn't leaving. He'd said what he felt needed to be said, and luckily she ignored him.

The sound of a car sent him stepping quickly to the side. It was Michael and panic about keeping the surprise sent everyone scattering like cockroaches when a light switch flipped on. Betty slammed the front door shut tightly as Piper pushed the cleaning supplies under the porch swing.

Jedda jogged up past Michael's car and joined everyone on the porch, forming a human shield from all the food that was wrapped and prepared in the house.

"I thought you all had the stomach bug." Michael looked them over. That was the lie Betty had told to keep he and Jules from popping in the house, but it clearly hadn't worked.

"We do," Betty said, clutching her stomach. "You best go on. I don't want you catching it and passing it to Jules and the baby."

"I wish I could go. But I need to talk to Jedda and Crystal. Now." Michael's face had a steely stare that shook Jedda's confidence in the security of his freedom.

"Everything okay?" Bobby asked, leaning himself against the porch railing and giving Michael a look.

"No," he replied dropping his eyes to his shoes.

"What's going on?" Betty asked folding her arms across her chest and tapping her foot expectantly.

"It's better if we talk in private," Michael said, waving for them to follow him. Jedda began down the steps but Crystal did not.

"No," Crystal said, her voice shaking.

"If you don't tell him I will," Michael asserted, his eyebrows high, daring her to test him.

"Tell him what?" Willow asked as she stepped out behind them. "What's going on?"

"I will tell him," Crystal managed to say. "But I'll tell him right here. I want everyone to hear my side of the story."

Jedda paused at the bottom of the porch steps and looked up at her as though he was staring at a stranger. What could she possibly have to admit? What secret had she been keeping from him?

"Suit yourself," Michael said, stepping behind Jedda and giving him a nudge forward. "I'm interested in hearing your side of the story too."

"What's happening here?" Piper asked, her face full of worry.

"I got a report yesterday that I'd been waiting for," Michael said, standing sternly in the corner of the porch. "I requested a list of anyone who'd received copies of the transcripts of Jedda's original trial or his history in foster care. I wanted to see if Brad's father was working against us. Crystal's name popped up on that list."

"So?" Jedda asked, looking over at her downturned face. "She was helping us. That's not a big deal."

"She requested the files, absolutely everything about your life, Willow's life, and your parents' life weeks before I ever bumped into her in the cafeteria of the courthouse. But she acted as though she knew nothing about any of it. She pretended you and your trial were news to her."

Jedda swallowed hard as he tried to reason away the information he was getting. So she lied about knowing more about him. Maybe she didn't want to come on too strong in her attempts to help.

"I'd like to hear why that is," Michael said, folding his arms across his chest and glaring at Crystal. Everyone was silent, waiting for her to speak. As she looked up, her eyes glassed over with tears.

"Who is it you were working for? What were they trying to do, get inside information about the case? Was it the news? Are you the one who led them to Willow?" Michael asked, sounding more like the one Jedda had grown accustomed to in court rather than the one on the porch.

"Are you serious?" Willow asked, charging forward. "You did this? You ruined my life? For what, they paid you or something? Is that why you're still here, feeding them more information? I knew there had to be a reason you were so interested in Jedda." Willow was nose to nose with Crystal looking ready to strike. Betty stepped forward and rested a hand on Willow's shoulder.

"You let her explain," Betty said decisively. "We aren't judge and jury here and the girl has a right to say her piece."

"I didn't talk to the news. No one was paying me anything," Crystal admitted as she used her thumbs to brush away her tears. "I heard your case was being reopened. I took interest in it at first because I remembered it from when I was a kid. I grew up a few miles from where you did. Just on the other side of Wheaton Park." Crystal fiddled with her necklace as she struggled to choke out her words.

"The nice houses?" Willow asked, and Jedda remembered it the same way. On the other side of the park were houses that were significantly better than their childhood home. It was a much nicer neighborhood of working class people.

"Yes," Crystal admitted, "I guess compared to where you guys grew up it would be considered nice. I remember when you killed your parents. So I started listening to the chatter going on about your case. Rumors started to go around about the trafficking ring your parents were involved in. After that I got all the records I could find on them and the both of you." She gestured to Jedda and Willow. "And then I made sure I stayed involved as more information came out."

"Stayed involved?" Jedda asked. "You mean you pretended to give a shit what happened to me. You acted like you cared?"

"I do care," Crystal said with a fierceness to her voice.

"You still haven't said why," Michael reiterated. "If not for money or because someone put you up to it, why did you need to get so close to this case? To Jedda?"

Crystal reached into her bag and pulled out a tattered photograph. "She was fourteen. My sister Erica. They called her a runaway but I never believed it. My sister told me everything, and if she were going to run away I'd have known about it. Back then there weren't abduction alerts. Things like this didn't make the news. No one cared that she went out one night and never came back. She'd been in trouble a couple times, shoplifting or something, and that was enough for them to write her off." Crystal ran her thumb across the edge of the picture and Jedda felt her pain even from the distance between them. "I dug into everything. Every case, every lead, all through my childhood I looked for an explanation. That's why I started interning at the courthouse and then got the job I did. I wanted access to information. I wanted to network with people who could help me when the time came. When I heard the details of your parents' crimes, the timeline fit. The location fit. My sister was spending all her time in your neighborhood, hanging with people who lived a few buildings away from you. I thought maybe there was a connection." Crystal turned the picture so Jedda could see it.

"Please tell me, do you recognize her? Was she ever in your house? Did you ever see her around there?" The tears were falling like a river from her eyes and Jedda felt his heart well into his throat. Crystal turned and faced Willow. "Please, I'm sorry that I lied to you but I need to find her. I need to know what happened."

Willow shook her head, looking to everyone else for help, as though she wished she weren't the closest one to Crystal anymore. "I'm sorry," Willow said, focusing on the picture. "I don't remember her. I don't think I've ever seen her."

Crystal looked over to Jedda with a pain in her eyes he wouldn't wish on anyone.

"I'm sorry too," he said, examining the picture. "I don't know her. I've never seen her."

Crystal held the picture to her chest and collapsed back into the chair with a sob that couldn't be calmed. Willow stepped back tentatively with a look that said she thought the sadness could be contagious, and she didn't want to catch it.

"It's okay, dear," Betty said, pulling Crystal into her arms. "I know you were counting on that. I'm sure that felt like your last chance, but as long as you keep up hope there is always something to hold onto."

"I really thought th-this c-c-could be it . . .," she stuttered out as she tried to catch her breath. "I'm so sorry I didn't tell you sooner. I was afraid of what you might think. People—they've called me crazy over the years—they say I'm obsessed. I just need to know she's alive."

"If you'd have told me, Crystal," Michael said, clearly shaken by her emotion but trying to stay on track, "I would have gladly shown them both the picture. I would have listened to you, and helped you. You didn't need to go through this whole charade. Did you really get fired, or was that a ploy to come down here?"

"I really got fired, but I planned to come down in a week or so anyway even if that didn't happen. I didn't know what else was going on down here, what Brad had going on. But for me it wasn't an act," Crystal said, gathering herself and trying to speak with a steady voice. "I did care about what happened to Jedda. I do believe he deserves to be free. Every minute I've spent with you has not been some show I'm putting on. All of you have to believe that."

Betty stroked her hair and nodded her head. "I believe you, sweetheart. You're a very genuine girl, but you've got a lot of pain in there that can make you do reckless things. I understand, and I believe you."

"I don't understand," Michael said, throwing his hands up in exasperation. "But I also don't think you're a terrible person. I just wish you'd have told me."

Willow, Piper, Bobby, and Clay remained quiet as every eye, including Crystal's, turned toward Jedda.

"You should go," he said flatly as he headed back into the house. "You asked what you needed to, got your answer, and now you should go."

"Jedda please, I care about you. You have to believe me," Crystal called, but her words were cut short by the slamming of the door.

Chapter Fourteen

"It's wedding day!" Betty chirped as she danced around the kitchen scooping grits onto everyone's plate. The tension in the house since yesterday's revelation was thick and unavoidable in the small space.

The arbor in the field out back had been erected and woven with flowers and paper-white tulle. The chairs were stacked and ready to set up. The food was all prepped and waiting to heat and serve. No guests had canceled, which Betty said she was taking as a good sign. That meant twenty-seven of their closest friends were overlooking the jabbering jaws of Edenville and pledging their allegiance to Betty. It wasn't even close to the ninety-five who had originally been invited, but Betty kept saying she was happy that they'd weeded the garden and pulled out all the snakes as well. Jedda liked that metaphor and he felt like, as of yesterday, his own garden had been cleaned out.

"I wasn't going to say anything, young lady, but I haven't heard you practicing any songs. Should I be worried?" Betty asked as she slid bacon onto Willow's plate then quickly snatched it back remembering she was a vegetarian. "Oh, my mistake, I forgot you don't eat anything that tastes good."

"I worked at a piano bar for two years. I can play every love song known to man and I can sing them in my sleep. You just make sure the guitar is ready for me to tune and I'll take care of the rest," Willow said, clearly attempting to lighten the mood of the house.

"I'm looking forward to hearing you sing," Clay said, as he poured everyone another round of coffee. He too had spent his morning trying to keep things from getting too tense. He did a lot of that. Either trying to rein in Betty or defuse some volatile situation. "It's going to be great having your help out there, Jedda. I was really impressed with your skills in the kitchen yesterday. You've got a gift, and when Betty and I get our restaurant up and going, there will certainly be a place for you there."

"Thanks, Clay," Jedda said, sipping at his coffee. He looked over at the empty chair Crystal had been occupying the last few days and felt a knot in his stomach. He was struggling to separate the ghost of a broken-hearted woman who fell to pieces on the porch yesterday from the person who'd lied in order to get close to him. He shook off his conflicted thoughts and tried to remember today was a day for celebration.

"Hurry up and shovel that food in, y'all. We have a full day of work and setup to do. Bobby and Piper should be here any minute." Betty was buzzing with energy as she started pulling plates out from under still-moving forks.

* * * *

The morning seemed to fly by as everything started to fall into place. The group, now joined by Piper and Bobby, had accomplished all they had set out to do. The tent, which was larger than they had anticipated, was the most difficult task so far. Bobby had been slapped across the face with a pole that had come loose from its slot. The welt by his eyes would surely look worse by the time he'd need to stand up as best man, but he continued to refuse the makeup Betty kept trying to smear across his face.

As Jedda stepped into the beautiful field, alive with the birth of spring, he saw his sister strumming the strings of a guitar Betty had pulled down from the attic. It had belonged to Stan. He could tell earlier that morning as Betty handed it over to Willow the connection she had to it. He was relieved that, in spite of Willow's mood, she was kind about it. She let Betty know how beautiful the guitar was and that she'd take good care of it while it was in her possession. It was a small insight into the person Willow truly was.

"Hey, kid," he said as he took a seat in next to her, "I think it's really nice that you're going to sing. It's going to be a special day for them. I feel badly that they've had to put if off as long as they have for me."

"Should be great," Willow said with more attitude than Jedda had hoped to hear. She rested the guitar across her chair and stood, looking as though she was trying to escape.

"Looks like we both got mixed up with the wrong people. I'm sorry you are dealing with this Brad shit. But I really believe Michael will figure it out and you can go back to your normal life. Back to all the good stuff."

"Yep. It really was a wonderful life. You're right about that. I shouldn't have a complaint in the world. I have about the best adoptive parents anyone could ask for. Every Christmas there were dozens of presents under the tree with my name on them. My birthday parties were like fairy tale dreams come true. I had it all, Jedda, and all it cost me was my brother. A pretty fair trade, wouldn't you say? I should be happy." Willow fumed, anger seething through her gritted teeth.

"I don't understand. Are you mad at what I did? Do you wish I just left you there? I didn't have a choice. I had to kill them, it was the only way I knew how to save you."

"Listen, if last night proved anything to me, it's that we're all pretty much on our own. If a girl like Crystal can be, well, what she was, then who can you trust? I don't want to get into all of our stuff today. I just want to get through this wedding and get on with my life."

"You're leaving again?"

"You're going to be fine down here. You don't need me, or the problems I bring with me. I can figure this out on my own and you'll be better for it."

"We can talk more later. It'll work out, I promise. I won't let anything happen to you," Jedda said, reaching for Willow, who pulled away and quickly slammed her hands to her head in sheer frustration.

"What's going on?" Bobby asked as he headed toward them with a folding table under his arm. "You okay, Willow?" He dropped the table and pulled her into his arms, holding her hands down so she couldn't strike her head again. She rested her tired head there for a moment and then shoved him backward as she righted herself.

"I'm fine. Okay? I'm great. I'm going to sit up here and sing at this wedding. This surprise wedding that is probably going to turn into a disaster when the bride finds out, since she said she didn't want it. Don't you people ever listen to what someone is saying to you? Don't you ever think that maybe she knows what's best for her?"

Her voice was loud and easily heard by an approaching Betty. "Dear, I'm going to pretend we're still talking about my daughter here and answer your question regardless of whether you intended it as rhetorical. Sometimes people say one thing. They say what they think people need to hear, when in fact their heart is begging for something else. And if you know that person as deeply as I know my daughter then you see through the words and you look into their soul. Jules will stand up here today before her friends and her family, next to the man she loves with all her heart, and do something she wants so badly to do. She'll look over at you playing her daddy's guitar and feel his presence here. She'll turn to me, see the tears in my eyes, and realize that even when she feels completely overwhelmed and misunderstood, someone can hear what her heart wants. She'll see Piper standing next to her, and Bobby next to Michael, and she'll know that she has fiercely loyal friends who will never let her fall. She won't see that the napkins weren't the ones she picked out and she won't notice all the people who didn't come. Instead she'll be warmed by all the people who did show up. Sometimes you need folks to ignore what you're saying and pay attention to what you need instead."

Willow's lips were stiffly pursed together as she listened to the speech. Jedda's heart was tightening as he wondered what his sister might shoot back. Would she embrace this moment or would she ruin it all with a snarky, defensive retort.

"That's nice, Betty, and I'm sure you're right about Jules. But that's because you know her so well. No one here knows me at all. So all that doesn't apply. You can't see through my words and get to what I really want, because no one here could ever understand what it feels like. So please, can we just go back to getting ready for this day and move on?" Willow asked meekly, raising her eyebrows at everyone expectantly.

"That's fine, dear," Betty whispered as she stepped closer to Willow and pulled her in for a hug. "I don't understand you, sweetheart, but I'm going to keep trying." She leaned away and looked into Willow's eyes. "I promise. I'll keep trying."

Jedda watched as Willow swallowed back the threat of tears and nodded her head, reluctant and grateful all at once.

"Now," Betty said loudly as she clapped her hands together, "it's time to call the bride and groom and trick them into coming to their wedding."

Betty hustled back down the path toward the house and, on the way, passed Josh, who was looking sheepish. Jedda watched as Betty patted him lightly on the back on her way by, and he instantly filled with relief, a skip returning to his step. He'd received a silent pardon from the queen.

"Hey Josh," Bobby said as he waved him over and gestured for him to help with the tables. "You're just in time for the manual labor."

"Great." Josh rolled up the sleeves of his sweatshirt. "I'm hoping if I do enough now I won't really have to do all the dishes later."

"Fat chance," Bobby groaned, "she's already got a set of dish gloves with your name on them. Literally, she wrote your name on them."

* * * *

When Michael and Jules pulled up to the house, the army of people standing there did a terrible job of holding poker faces. The fact that all the girls had their hair in updos didn't help either. Willow was trying to pay attention to their arrival but she felt herself distracted as she replayed her conversation with Jedda. She wondered if Betty's prediction of Jules's reaction to the surprise would come to fruition. She wondered if her swirling conflicted feelings she held about herself and her brother would ever settle long enough for Betty to truly understand, the way she promised she would.

"What's wrong with all of you?" Jules asked as Bobby opened her car door and let her use him as leverage to get her body to a standing position.

"Nothing wrong with us," Betty said, pushing Bobby out of the way and pulling her daughter into her arms. "You can't have anything wrong with you on your daughter's wedding day."

"My what?" Jules asked, looking over her mother's shoulder at Piper whose grin was uncharacteristically wide.

"Today is your wedding day," Betty squealed, releasing her daughter from a tight hug and pulling her by the hand toward the house. "Now, Michael your tux is hanging there on the porch. You and the boys will get ready in the shed. I don't want you seeing the blushing bride in her dress. It's bad luck."

"Ma," Jules said, pulling her hand away and stopping in her tracks. "My dress doesn't fit. This won't work. Please tell me you didn't plan a wedding for today."

"Crystal altered it," Jedda said, feeling everyone's eyes on him at the sound of her name.

"She's not here?" Jules asked, looking around. "Michael told me what happened. He told me about her sister. She'll be here today right?"

"I told her she should go," Jedda said, brushing some stray dirt off his sleeve. "That was last night. I didn't specifically tell her not to come today, but I'm sure she's on her way back to New York by now."

"Well I hope she comes. She's been through a lot and she's a mighty nice girl. No matter what way you slice it, she helped you and Michael out in New York, and that counts for something," Jules said, rubbing at her aching back. "Where are we having this thing? In the kitchen?" Jules's face was filled with confusion.

"That's a surprise, dear. You just have to get yourself looking like a stunning bride and the rest is all taken care of."

"So we're going to be married before the baby comes?" Jules asked, clasping her hands over her mouth to hold in a squeal of excitement.

Betty's eyes were wet with tears as she answered, "As long as she can wait another three hours, then yes."

"I can't believe this, Ma, this is like a surprise party, but it's a wedding," Jules exclaimed, sinking into Michael's arms. He smiled down at his soon-to-be bride, looking pleased to know she was happy.

"That's right," Betty said victoriously. "It's a surprise wedding. I invented it."

Willow averted her eyes from the scene, and found herself looking in Josh's direction instead. He'd come up to stand beside her. "I really thought that was going to be more exciting," he said in a low voice, leaning down toward her ear. The smell of his cologne wafted toward her and she found herself caught up in it for a moment before she could speak.

"Yeah," she finally answered. "I guess we were wrong. Apparently some people really do like surprises."

"The only thing I hate more than surprises is being wrong. So today I'm batting a thousand," Josh said, smiling only after he saw Willow's mouth turn up slightly.

"We've got a lot left to do to get this bride ready," Betty announced as she ushered the girls onto the porch. "Clay, you and the men don't take nearly as long to prepare so you finish up everything for the ceremony and keep an eye on the food. Mrs. Clarice will be here with the cake in an hour. Guests will be arriving an hour after that." Betty pulled her daughter through the door with the excitement of a child on Christmas morning.

Willow trailed in the house behind them, turning to look over her shoulder at Josh who was heading back down the yard toward the path that led to the field.

"He's good looking," Piper said as she held the door open for Willow. "He seems to like you."

"Then he's misjudged me." Willow shrugged off the idea like it was an accusation. "But it's not his fault, it happens all the time."

Chapter Fifteen

The cake arrived right on time and the guests trickled in slowly as the afternoon approached. Jedda sat nervously in the front row of chairs feeling like every eye was on him. Hopefully the bride would be out soon and she'd pull all the attention she deserved her way instead. Bobby had loaned him a button-down shirt, a pair of khakis, and sport coat that was a little too short in the sleeves, but significantly more appropriate than anything he owned.

Michael and Bobby stood to the right of the arbor, both wearing gray suits with icy blue ties. With their hair tamed with gel and their faces clean-shaven, they stood chatting casually as if today were any other day in their happy lives.

Jedda watched as Bobby disappeared from his post next to Michael and headed to the house. Things were probably about to start any minute and he kept looking down at the two empty seats beside him—one for his sister and one for Crystal.

Willow appeared and settled into her seat and that left Jedda looking down at the last empty one. Willow looked more grown-up and polished than he'd ever seen her. Her hair was pulled up in an intricate knot, and she wore a flowery dress that Betty had pulled from Jules's left-behind clothes.

Without a word, Crystal appeared and slipped into the chair next to him. She was wearing a strapless cotton dress in a pale green that suited her ivory skin perfectly. Her hair was half up, with little white flowers tucked around the edges of a braid that twisted back around her head. Her lips were a glossy pink and her nails a matching shade. She looked amazing, but there was something missing—an accessory she always wore, but not today—her smile. The bubbly, effervescent smile that, in Betty's words, you could see from the moon on a clear night. He'd told her to go, yet here she was.

"I didn't think you'd come," Jedda said in a hushed voice. "I figured you'd be on your way to New York."

"The only thing you didn't know about me, you found out yesterday. Everything else I've ever been, everything I've ever said, has been absolutely and authentically me. And if you believed that then you'd know I was up at the house making sure that dress fit Jules. And that I wouldn't miss the magic and happiness of someone's wedding for anything. That's who I am."

Jedda searched for words as the music began to flow through the speakers that Josh had set up. Every head turned toward the path leading back to the house. Piper, holding a bouquet of wild flowers plucked right from the field they all stood in, was heading slowly to the arbor where Michael was standing. Her smile was small, her eyes staring straight ahead. She wore a beautiful gown in the same ice blue of the ties Michael and Bobby were wearing.

Coming down behind Piper was Betty, her arm locked with Clay's. They looked like a dapper couple both beaming with joy. Unlike Piper, Betty's eye seemed to connect with everyone she passed, a knowing nod, a kind smile. Betty's hair was down for the first time since Jedda had met her, only the sides pulled back and pinned up. If anyone could burst with pride, physically explode from it, surely Betty was about to.

As the bridal march began to play, everyone stood. At the head of the aisle was a radiant Jules, her arm locked solidly with Bobby's. The tears were already visible in her eyes as she looked over the people who'd come to celebrate, the work that had been put into the preparation, and the perfect spot that had been selected. Jedda was happy for Jules and Michael today, but as he looked over at Bobby he felt tears in his own eyes. He'd worried what his choices had done to the people around him. He disrupted Bobby's life when he committed those murders. Bobby and his parents had taken him in, given him everything, and all he gave back was chaos. But today, watching who he'd become with this amazing group of people, Jedda felt relieved. Jules was Bobby's best friend, his savior in the wake of what Jedda had done. And today, taking the spot of her late father, he was here to give his friend away. Jedda hadn't done much talking to God in his life, but at that moment his gratitude was being silently sent up to the sky with a chant of Thank you. Thank you for making sure people survived my actions. Thank you for letting me see this day. Thank you for giving me another chance.

As Bobby and Jules reached the front of the guests, Michael reached out a hand to his best man but quickly opted for a hug instead. The men embraced tightly and Bobby took his place next to him while Michael took a second to take in the stunning woman he was about to commit himself to. He leaned in and kissed her cheek, then leaned down and kissed her round belly.

The minister held up a hand to quiet the coos and laughter as he spoke. "Dearly beloved," he began, and just like that, two people became one, and Jedda felt eternally blessed to be able to witness it.

Michael cleared his throat as he began to say the vows he'd written. Though they didn't have much time to prepare for the wedding, Michael had no problem penning his vows quickly. He had clearly known what he wanted to say to his future wife. "Jules, when people look at you, I think they might assume you're crazy." He said it with a smile, and all the guests gasped and chuckled. "You've got a wild temper. You hardly ever listen to sage advice, and you're quick to fight. When I first met you, that's what I saw. That's what I believed about you. But then I started to see the truth. Your temper was really just the expression of your passion for what you believe. You know yourself well, and you know your convictions. I now see your reactions as a fervent defending of who you are at the moment you're challenged. Not listening to sound advice, I understand, is an element of your free spirit. You leap before you look and occasionally the fall is farther than you thought, but more often than not, you arrive first in the most amazing places while the rest of us are still working up the courage to jump. And your quick response to fight, I recognize completely as your fierce protection of those you love. I've never seen you attack for your own preservation, but always for the people around you. So I think when people look at you, they think you're crazy, because I did. But I am so glad I looked closer, because now I see in you all the things I hope are passed down to our daughter. She'd be lucky to be as crazy as you are."

Jules's face was like stone as she took in Michael's words. He'd taken a risk for sure; anyone who was watching could see that. After a long moment Jules began to speak, still not letting her face show a reaction to his vows.

"Michael, I had vows written for you here. They were all about how much I love you and how I would do anything for you. But I'm not going to say those vows anymore." Jedda realized too late he was holding his breath and had to gasp slightly to keep from passing out. The suspense was on the verge of killing him. "Instead of me telling you how much I love you, I think it's better if I tell you how much your love means to me. I feel like I've waited my whole life for someone to look at me that closely. I've waited all this time for someone to see me the way you just described. I've finally found the man who can love this kind of crazy, and it's how I know I'm right where I belong today. So you're right, people might think I'm loony, but as long as you can tell the difference, I know I'm with the right man."

When the words "you may kiss the bride" rang out loudly across the open field, everyone erupted in cheers, and the event turned quickly from a ceremony to a party. Jedda raced off to finish prepping the food with Clay. It was something he enjoyed more than he ever imagined. Clay was brilliant in the kitchen and all the reading Jedda had done had him feeling more knowledgeable than he thought he would be. Clay made numerous comments about how impressed he was. Sure, he was only chopping onions and shredding cabbage but, still, for the first time he felt skilled at something and it filled him with pride.

Willow and Josh were in charge of the music. Together they worked out when Willow would sing as well as the list of songs that would play when she wasn't.

When the food was served, the "first" dances done, and music played softly in the background, the pinging of a knife on the side of a wine glass drew everyone's attention.

Bobby stood up from his spot next to Michael at the long table and began to speak. "We're going to do things a little differently here. But this is Betty's house so you should all be used to that by now. Normally the best man would give a toast directed at the groom, and while I have a hundred things I could say to him, I've got a million to say to Jules. So that's who my toast is for."

Jules covered her heart with her hand as her chin quivered with emotion. "Don't get too mushy, Bobby. With these hormones I'm likely to flood this tent with tears."

"Jules, you are my longest lasting friendship. It's impossible for me to look back over the last fifteen years and not think of you. We made our share of mistakes together, we've fought and we've disagreed but we've never let go of each other. Even when it would have been the easiest thing for us to do. You're here with Michael today, and I'm lucky enough to be here with Piper. They've both made us the best versions of ourselves. They've both challenged us to grow and change in ways we desperately needed. I love them for that. But I love you, because before I was ready to be this grown-up, well-rounded person, you loved me. You loved the kid who showed up here and didn't know what to do with himself. You loved the teenager who thought he could control everything. You loved the guy who chose to be a cop, even when it scared you. You never let me go, even when I gave you reasons to. And I'm never going to let you go. That little girl," Bobby said, choking on his emotions as he gestured toward Jules's belly, "will have the most wildly protective, dedicated, and loving godfather in the world. The two of you will be incredible parents and with any luck . . ." Bobby said, gathering himself and plastering on a devilish smile, "little Françoise will have Jules's looks but not her temper."

"Yes!" Betty shouted, as she stood and slapped Bobby on the shoulder. "I knew I'd get more people in the Françoise camp."

Jules stood and pulled Bobby in for a playfully forceful hug. "I should have known you couldn't be sweet for that long. You'd have to end on a sour note."

Another round of clinking glasses led to Piper standing up to deliver a toast of her own. "Since Bobby covered the toast for Jules, I thought I should give my friend Michael his. Michael is literally the first person in this town who I connected with. As many of you know by now, coming to Edenville was a difficult journey for me and I didn't think I'd ever feel comfortable here, but Michael was the first to give me hope that it might happen one day. I think we'd all like to believe we have a plan for ourselves. If we work hard and act strategically we can carve our way through this world. We can forge our own path, and nothing can stop us. For me, I never really believed in a higher power out there having a plan for us."

Betty cleared her throat and made a sign of the cross. "I'm still working on it," she said to the minister who was sitting at the table to her left.

Piper rolled her eyes and continued, "I mean I didn't used to believe that. But now when I sit here and look at the four of us, I think there must be someone in our corner. How could four people start where we started and end up here unless someone was guiding us? Michael, the kindness you showed to me before I really earned it is a testament to who you are and the kind of husband and father you will be. You are one of the most fearless and loyal people I've ever met in my life, and as I watch you move through this world and continue to make it better, I realize how lucky I am to know you. The first night I brought you here, I couldn't have imagined it would lead to a day as amazing as today. And that's how I know this was all meant to be, that every moment led us here. Because not in our wildest dreams did we think this was in store for us, but here we are. And I don't think any of us would trade it for the plans we thought we wanted." Piper raised her glass in the air and the crowd followed her lead. "To the best laid plans, and how wonderful it is when they go awry."

Michael stood and hugged Piper and then leaned down and kissed his wife. From the other side of the tent, the strum of a guitar drew everyone's attention. Willow's soft low voice began a song about love that immediately quieted the entire field. Even the crickets, just starting their dusk chirping, seemed to stop and listen. The lyrics were unfamiliar but at the same time felt as though they'd been sung a hundred times before. It only took a moment for Jedda to realize this was an original song, something Willow had written. The reason he felt he already knew it was because it was what Willow would sound like if she herself were a song. It was equal parts of joy and longing. Quiet and piercing.

It was met with nodding heads and broad smiles from everyone who stepped out onto the makeshift dance floor wrapping their arms around each other and swaying to the beat of Willow's heart as she strummed her soul out. Jedda looked over at Crystal who was mesmerized by his sister's talent. "She's incredible," she whispered.

"She could sing when we were little," Jedda said as he stood to step away from Crystal.

"I'm sorry, Jedda," she said, the tears in her eyes forming again.

"It's all right. As a matter of fact, I feel a little relieved. I was falling for you. And I just kept reminding myself how bad of an idea that was. How much I'd probably just destroy you. I actually feel relieved that you don't want more from me."

"I do," Crystal said in a raspy emotional voice. "That wasn't an act, Jedda. I do want you. Us."

Jedda placed his napkin on his plate and closed his eyes for a moment, trying to center himself. He could feel his grip on his anger toward her fading, and that scared him. Without another word he turned and walked away.

Chapter Sixteen

The late afternoon had turned into dusk, and then nightfall, but nothing could take them away from the field tonight. Crystal had headed to the house to help clean up, trying to give Jedda some space but clearly not wanting to leave. The lanterns Bobby had brought down from the shed were enough for them to huddle around in their circle of chairs. The tall trees cast shadows of moonlight all around them. The stars sparkled like nothing Jedda had ever seen before. Fireflies danced across the dark corners of the field. They'd all had their share of wine and champagne, of laughs and tears, and now all that was left to do was sit and take in the serenity of a southern night, surrounded by woods.

Even Josh and Willow seemed to be getting along well enough. She was sitting off to the side with him as he strummed the guitar and she hummed a song. Jedda felt lightness in his heart every time he heard her laugh at something Josh was saying. He liked the way Josh looked at his sister. All he wanted was for Willow to be happy, that's all he could ever remember wanting. So much of life didn't make sense to him. What made a man like Brad so set on hurting others for sport? What kept his sister from enjoying the life right in front of her, the one she'd been given? Why, if Crystal was only pretending to care about him, was she still here? But just as his hopes had risen for Willow, they were quickly dashed as Josh leaned in to kiss her and she shot up like a firecracker, scrambling to get as far from him as possible.

Jedda fought the instinct to go to her when Willow raised her voice. Although she quickly dropped it to a quieter level, it was too late to avoid an audience. "Oh,

Willow," Jedda sighed, dropping his head to his hands. Everyone had already seen the commotion and, like usual, it was up to Betty to do something.

"Did y'all hear that noise in the woods? We need to get this food out of here before the critters come to rummage through it. Josh and Bobby, you grab those two tables there. Everyone, gather an armful of food or dishes and head up to the house. Jedda and Willow, you stay down here and clear off the cake table," Betty directed, moving everyone along with the waving of her hands as though she were conducting an orchestra. Her calculated move to give Willow and Jedda some time to talk was blatant, but no one had the nerve to call her on it.

Jedda made his way quietly to the table where the mostly eaten cake sat, looking like a picked over carcass. He started scraping the remnants of frosting off the plates and into the trash as Willow joined him.

"He tried to kiss me," she said defensively as she rolled up the sleeves of her cardigan and started to help clear the table. The bruises had begun to heal, switching from deep purples to marbled greens and browns. Even as their intensity faded, Jedda's reaction to them was still as powerful as ever. They made rage course through him like a river cutting its way through a mountain.

"I know. And if you didn't want him to, then that's fine. I'm just worried that you're pushing everyone away. People who really want to help you. You've been acting strange for days, and I feel like it's more than just the Brad ordeal. That talk we had didn't make any sense to me. I just imagined we'd have more to say to each other."

"I don't have anything to say. I don't want to talk it out. I don't want you to tell me the right answer."

"So what do you want?" he asked, his tone rougher than he intended.

"I don't know. I want to feel better. I want to be happy. I want to forgive you and forgive myself, but it's not that easy."

"Happy? You aren't happy?" Her reaction to those words tore a hole in Jedda's heart. Her chin quivered and her lower lip buckled beneath the weight of her emotions.

"Sorry to disappoint you," she snapped, tossing more cake into the trash.

A rustling behind Jedda had Willow wiping quickly at her eyes and getting her emotions in check. He assumed someone was coming back for another load of trash or to help them wrap up the cake. But he was wrong, and the look on his sister's face made that perfectly clear.

"How l-lucky can I g-g-get?" Brad asked in a slurred stutter. "I've been waiting to get the two of you alone for a while, and here you are. And even better, we're out in the woods."

Jedda turned quickly and swiped the large serrated cake knife off the table. "Go," is all he said as he backed up toward Willow and wielded the knife confidently.

"Perfect," Brad chuckled franticly, "a knife. That would be assault with a deadly weapon. That would seal your fate for sure."

"Or I could slit your throat and it would seal your fate," Jedda growled, pushing Willow behind him.

"He's trained in martial arts, Jedda. Don't let him fool you. He can hold his own and he's high on something," Willow warned.

"Well let's go then, come at me," Brad taunted, signaling with his hands that he was ready for a fight. "Let's get you thrown back in jail."

"I'm not going to attack you," Jedda said defiantly. "You can do and say whatever you want from over there, but I'm not playing your game."

"Oh, so she didn't tell you yet?" Brad asked, hitting his hand to his forehead feigning absentmindedness. "Because if she had you'd already be over here trying to kill me. Tell him what really happened, Willow. Tell him about those bruises."

"Shut up, Brad," Willow snapped as she dug her hands into Jedda's arm then whispered to him, "Let's make a run for the house, we'll go through the woods."

Jedda shook her off and gripped the knife even tighter. "I already know you beat her up. You found out about who she is and you attacked her."

"Well, not really," Brad said, jumping forward and acting as though he might strike, and then stepping back and laughing obsessively. "I was pissed when I found out she was a filthy whore. I certainly couldn't date her anymore—wouldn't even be seen in public with her if my life depended on it." He made a face of disgust as he kicked a folding chair, launching it in their direction. Jedda deflected it with his arm and again tucked Willow farther behind him. "But then I realized something." Brad winced. "A freak like that, she might not be anyone I'd like on my arm at a dinner party but she might be fun in my bed. She'd like it rough. I mean, even the news said she was found chained to the wall. I could tie her up. I could burn her or bruise her and it would turn her on." He licked at his lips and then pursed them into a kiss as he winked at Willow. "The same way I liked to read comic books when I was that age, getting smacked around would be nostalgic for her." He spit in their direction and Jedda felt the spray hit his face. His fury was building to a tipping point, as the look in Brad's eye grew even more crazed. "So I didn't beat the crap out of her to punish her, I did it while screwing her, 'cause I knew she'd like it."

A blind, black rage hit Jedda harder than any punch he'd ever received. It socked him in the chest so hard he actually felt the need to take a step back, leaning slightly on Willow.

"You didn't!" Jedda demanded as he got his footing and raised the knife up higher, the moon catching it and glistening across Brad's manic face.

"No," Willow cried as she looped her arms around Jedda's bicep. "He didn't. He didn't, Jedda. I got away from him. I fought him off."

"She's right. The bitch locked herself in the bathroom until I passed out. Then she ran off and ratted me out," Brad said, shrugging his shoulders. "But I never leave unfinished business. So I plan to get my fun in eventually. I'll have you screaming my name even if it's just to beg me to stop. Maybe sooner than you think." Brad took a step forward as Jedda raised the knife to strike down on him. A snapping twig behind him was enough to snag his mind and pull it back to reality. From the corner of his eyes he could see the shadows and outlines of the people who loved him. They were there, they were with him.

"We all heard what he said," Michael assured them as he took a step closer, slowly moving toward Jedda. "We heard what he did."

"Stop, Michael. Stop where you are and take Willow back to the house. I'm ending this."

In a flash someone blew past Jedda and he felt a hand plant hard onto his chest. It was Crystal and the fire flashing in her eyes was enough to catch Jedda's attention for a brief second. Long enough for him to stop the charge he was about to take forward.

"You're not doing this, Jedda. Things are different than they were before. You're not making the same choice. I won't let you."

"Nothing's different," Jedda bellowed, still unwilling to lower the knife. "He's no different than my parents. He's never going to stop until he destroys her."

"You're right," she agreed, keeping her palm planted on Jedda's chest, pushing back as he leaned forward. "He's a monster and so were they. The things he said, what he did to her, he's evil."

"So nothing's different. I'm not different. I'm the same person. I feel the same way right now as I did that day and I'll do the same thing. I'll do whatever I have to do to protect her. If this is going to send me back to prison, then that is where I belong. I'm no different. Nothing has changed."

"Fine," Crystal said, putting her hand on his cheek and pulling his eyes down to hers. "Fine, you're the same guy. You killed for her and you'd do it again. You're the same guy."

"Then move. Let me end this," Jedda said angrily, narrowing his eyes at Brad, clenching the knife even harder.

"He's the same as your parents, and you're the same as the kid who killed them, but something has changed Jedda. If you could see the army of people standing behind you, you would understand what I mean. Back then, it was just you, alone. Willow, alone. You had no one to turn to, no one to depend on. That's what's different now. Look behind you. You're not in this alone. You've got a cop in your corner, a lawyer, a crazy-ass redhead, an old lady with a shotgun, and a sister who needs you out here. And right here in front of you, you have a woman who's in love with you. Even if you don't believe that, it's true. Last time you stood like this, ready to change your life forever to save your sister, you had no help and no hope for a future. That's what's changed. That's what's different."

He locked eyes with Crystal and searched her face, trying to discern the truth from fiction. It wasn't easy to trust. She'd betrayed him, there was no way around that. But she was still here. She was standing between him and a life changing decision. She didn't fear him or the knife in his hand. Could that be anything but real love?

Jedda took in a deep breath as he slowly lowered the knife and turned his head to see the group standing behind him. Their faces were a mix of worry and hopefulness that settled somewhere around relief. Crystal was right. This was different. He was the same, the danger was the same, but the circumstance gave him options he'd never had before.

Michael leaned in and took the knife from Jedda's lowered hand and guided him backward.

"Are you kidding me?" Brad shouted as he reached forward and grabbed a handful of Crystal's hair, yanking her backward into his arms. Her yelp drew everyone's eyes and Bobby charged forward, stopping when he saw the small knife pressed against her neck. He drew his service weapon and steadily pointed it at Brad's head. Brad shifted quickly putting Crystal in the line of fire, ducking behind her.

"Get your hands off her or I'll make a mess your daddy can't clean up," Bobby hissed.

"I have all the power," Brad barked. "Here and everywhere." He twisted Crystal's body left and right as he shouted out to them. "You are like ants in my world."

"He's tweaking out on something," Willow yelled as she stepped forward to Bobby's side, slipping past everyone's pawing arms that had attempted to pull her back.

"Listen kid," Bobby said, steadying his voice and relying on his training, "you're right. You have all the power. So tell me what you want."

"I-I-I," Brad stuttered. "I want her. I want her to come with me." He pointed at Willow. "She comes with me and gives me the laptop and I make sure she doesn't ever rat on me."

"Okay," Bobby said, nodding his head reassuringly. "Then that's what we'll do."

"No!" Jedda shouted, unwilling to let his sister become a bargaining chip in a crazy man's game.

Michael planted his hand on Jedda's shoulder and gave him a knowing look. "He's got this," he whispered.

"Willow will go with you. She'll get you the laptop," Bobby said as they all watched the blade press down harder into Crystal's tender flesh.

"Yeah?" Brad asked, his eye twitching as he tried to make sense of the scenario he'd created. Bobby nodded, gestured for him to let Crystal go as he nudged Willow forward a step.

"Take her, and she'll take you to the laptop."

As Brad slowly lowered his knife and loosened his grip on Crystal, Bobby charged forward, and with the butt of his gun, cracked Brad across the face, sending him falling to the ground. Both Crystal and Willow went tripping forward into the waiting arms of their circle of friends.

"Clay, go up to the house and get my cuffs. I'm arresting him for assault, public intoxication, and whatever else I can come up with," Bobby called, and Clay turned on his heels with Betty in tow and headed back to the house.

"You think this was my only play?" Brad asked, snickering through the fog of his slurred speech as the blood poured out of his nose. "My father deals in information, swapping dirt on people. He's dug up enough on you. Looks like you had to save your girlfriend from her own crazy-ass father. The reports say the guy pulled a gun, and you killed him. My father read those reports and he says they didn't add up. Your superiors weren't very interested in the inconsistencies though. Everyone was just so damn happy to have that mess she brought with her over. What would they find if they looked again? If they reopened the case and investigated further? How would you fare?"

Jedda watched as Bobby's jaw clenched and he swallowed hard, clearly affected by the words of this lunatic. "And your lawyer buddy?" Brad asked, thrusting his chin toward Michael. "There's a rumor that he might have orchestrated the flipping and protection of the most notorious crime boss in the state. The guy who turned on all his associates and then went into hiding. What do you think would happen if people found out he had a hand in that, and worse, that he might know how to find the guy. How safe do you think that baby of yours would be?"

"Go to hell," Jules snapped as she stepped forward wielding an empty champagne bottle in her hand like a weapon. Michael caught her wrist, and pulled the bottle back. In a hushed voice he calmed her.

Clay hustled back past everyone and tossed the handcuffs to Bobby, who began to clasp them on.

"Stop," Willow said flatly. "Let him go." She stepped forward and Jedda could feel his blood start rushing again, seeing his sister so close to Brad.

"What are you talking about?" Bobby asked, halting momentarily to hear her out.

"Let him go, and I'll make the deal with his father. I'll give him the laptop. I'll sign something that says I'll never say anything. Whatever he wants."

"I knew you'd come to your senses," Brad grinned, winking in her direction.

"No way. He just assaulted Crystal. This isn't your call, it's up to her if she wants to press charges," Bobby said, looking over at Crystal for support.

Jedda assumed her answer would be swift and decisive, but instead she hesitated.

Willow spoke up instead. "I'm not going to watch him dismantle everyone's life one block at a time. The things he's saying about you both, whether they are true or not, it would cause you serious trouble. I'm not letting it happen. Not when getting him to stop is within my control. If you arrest him right now, you're throwing down the gauntlet and we'll have no chance at making any of this go away. Just let him go, and I'll make the deal."

"I want to know what he did," Bobby insisted. "Before I decide anything, I want to know what's on the laptop and what crime we'd be letting him walk away from."

"No," Willow protested. "It doesn't matter. Whatever he did, it won't change what he'd do to all of you if you push it any further."

"I want to hear it, Willow," Bobby insisted. Willow remained silent.

"You know why she doesn't want you to know," Brad said flatly. "She's not as innocent as she wants you to believe. I couldn't have pulled any of it off without her." Bobby jerked Brad's head backward, yanking a handful of his hair.

Michael cut in. "He sold drugs out of his dorm. He got greedy and started dealing some expensive synthetic stuff that put a few kids in the hospital. One of them isn't expected to recover fully. He has some brain damage and motor skills problems now. He's the son of a senator. A politician who happens to be a good friend and cohort of Brad's father. If this guy finds out Brad is responsible for his son's condition it would undo a very tangled web of favors, bribery, and deals, and land Brad in prison."

Brad sneered over at Willow. "How do you think I got those drugs? Someone had to steal the ingredients. Good thing I was dating a girl whose dad was a doctor, and who blindly trusted her."

"Willow?" Jedda asked, a wave of disappointment and nausea flowing through him.

"It isn't what you think. That isn't what happened," Willow said, stumbling backward as she tried to distance herself from this moment.

"Is that why you wanted to run? Is that why you want to make a deal with this guy?" Bobby asked, shaking his head in disgust.

"No. That isn't why. I don't want him to hurt anyone. I don't want him to cause any of you any more problems."

"Did you steal the drugs from your father and give them to Brad?" Bobby asked as his nostrils flared with an anger he was trying to restrain.

"Yes," she said, all the blood draining from her face. "But let me explain."

"No," Michael said, raising his hand to stop her. "Don't say another word. Don't incriminate yourself any further. Bobby, let him go."

Everyone was silent, the hooting of an owl and chirping of crickets the only noises.

"There isn't much we can do here, Bobby. If you arrest him, there is no turning back. It's the start of a war. Willow supplied the raw material to make the drugs, she stole them, we'd be sending her to jail if we pursue this."

"Why were you going to let Michael build a case if you knew you'd be implicated? Did you just plan to run if it came to that?" Bobby asked.

"I planned to tell my side of the story. I planned to explain," Willow said, her voice small and shaking.

"That ship has sailed," Michael said like a disappointed parent.

"I still don't think we should let him go. We've fought plenty in the past. We'll do what we always do," Bobby said, slamming one of Brad's arms behind his back.

"This is different. This isn't last year and this guy isn't someone you cross without being ready for his response. Especially if the situation is compromised, which we now know it is."

"What's so different this year? We're talking about a guy who attacked Willow and Crystal. Even if she did do something wrong, she certainly didn't deserve that. He's made threats against your wife and child. You think he should be walking free?" Bobby asked.

"No, but I also have a hell of a lot more to lose than I ever had before and so do you," Michael reminded him. "If this goes on long enough, one way or another they'll get Jedda back behind bars."

Bobby bit at his lip and let out an aggravated low roar. "I can't believe we're even considering letting him go. How do we know he won't just come back?"

"I'll take care of it personally with his father," Michael promised. "I'll make sure the terms are clear and we're all protected in the future. I don't see any other choice now."

Bobby shoved Brad forward and tucked his cuffs away behind him. "I won't let you go a second time. Do you understand me? If this happens again—you come around, you threaten anyone, I don't care what you think you're capable of, I'll take you down myself."

"Smart choice, letting me go," Brad said as he passed Willow, running his hand across her cheek. "My father will be here tomorrow afternoon. Bring the laptop and he'll talk details with you." He grabbed a half full bottle of champagne as he headed for the path leading back to the house.

No one spoke as the lanterns started to burn dim and the air seemed to drop a few degrees. Even Betty seemed at a loss for words, and her uncharacteristic silence made the moment even more ominous. It was Jules who spoke first as she leaned over and took a handful of cake and brought it to her lips.

"I got married today," she said as she looped her free arm with her husband's, and pushed the cake into her mouth with her other hand.

"Me too," Michael grinned as he kissed his wife and rubbed her belly affectionately.

Jules turned toward Bobby. "There was more good than bad today. Sometimes that's all you can ask for."

"And sometimes that doesn't feel like enough," Bobby said as he wrapped his arm around Piper and headed for the house. His anger was palpable and Jedda imagined letting a guy like Brad go was torture for Bobby.

Chapter Seventeen

Willow felt Jedda's eyes on her as she went back to clearing the cake off plates as though nothing at all had happened.

"Why didn't you tell me?" he asked as he pulled a dirty plate from her hand. "Why didn't you tell me there was more to the story?"

"I didn't think anyone would understand or believe me if they heard my side of the story about the drugs. Now Michael's telling me to shut my mouth about it and no one even knows what really happened. He said once we're alone and I can invoke attorney client privileges, then I can tell him. But not tonight while he's been drinking."

"And now what? What happens next?"

"I think if I remember right, we all live happily ever fucking after," Willow snapped as she brushed the crumbs off her hands. "Is that what you need to hear? Can you please just go up there and talk to Crystal? She just told you she loves you. That has to mean something to you. Why are you here wasting your time trying to figure me out? Go work your own shit out."

"Jedda," Josh said, stepping forward. "It's been a crazy night, why don't you give her some space. I'll help her finish here."

"Come on," Piper said, pulling Jedda by the arm, "she'll be fine."

Willow shook her head and slammed another plate against the trashcan. "She'll be fine," she whispered angrily to herself.

"You don't have to be fine," said Josh, tying up the trash bag and reaching for another.

"Thanks," she shot back sarcastically. "I'll be fine once I get out of here. No one's talking me out of it this time. Tomorrow morning I'm going. I'm not going to have everyone here looking at me like a criminal. I'm not a criminal." She hesitated as she bit at her lip. "I'm going home."

"I believe you. I know Michael told you not to talk about it so don't, but for what it's worth I'm sure you do have a good explanation."

"I do. But why do you believe me?"

"I love music. I know a lot of people say that, but I mean it. I genuinely love music. I connect to it on a level most people don't understand. That first time I met you, when you sang that song to calm Jedda down, it struck me. Even just hearing you hum on the way home from the train station. The song you sang tonight, you wrote that, right?"

"Yes," Willow said, her eyes still turned down.

"You've got a soulfulness about you, and while I think you're caught up in your own head right now, I don't believe you're a criminal and I don't think you set out to hurt anyone."

"You can tell that from my songs?"

"I can tell by the way you talk to people. I can tell by the way you try to protect people even if that means leaving them. You have a good heart."

"Thanks. It doesn't change what everyone up at the house is thinking about me, but I appreciate it."

"I'm sorry about earlier. I had no business trying to kiss you. I underestimated what you were going through with Brad. What he had . . . done."

"Stop, please. That isn't why I didn't want you to kiss me. Okay? I just didn't want you to. Is that impossible to imagine, that a woman might not like you?"

"I guess there's a first for everything." Josh shrugged, and Willow rolled her eyes at his attempt at levity. She could appreciate the fact that he was trying.

"I'm sure a lot of girls like you. If things were different I can see how there might be something between us. But it's pointless. Especially since I'm leaving."

"You could come back, right? Just because you're leaving now doesn't mean you won't ever be back."

"I guess there's a chance of it. I don't know." Willow shifted uncomfortably as she saw where this conversation was heading. She prayed he wouldn't be an idiot, but she knew it was coming.

"So I could wait. I could see if you come back," Josh said as he shook open the trash bag.

"Are you kidding me?" Willow slammed down a dish, her eyes wide with disbelief.

"I'm not proposing marriage or anything, I'm just saying, if you needed some time to get yourself squared away, I think you're worth waiting for."

"If you can't understand why that statement bothers me so much then we have nothing left to talk about. Don't wait for me. Don't put your damn life on hold for me."

"I don't understand. Every time I think I'm saying the right thing to you, it ends up being the wrong thing. So maybe shed some light on it for me."

"Do you think I need one more person in my life being a martyr? Someone else putting their life on hold, putting themselves second to me? Even when I continue to screw it up and make it worse. Even when I'm clearly not worthy of that sacrifice. Take a look around, Josh. That position's already been filled, and there seems to be a line of applicants behind him. And the fact that you even offered, tells me you have no idea what I need."

"That might be the only thing we have in common, because I don't think you have any idea what you need either. What a hardship for you, all this kindness and friendship. I just don't know how you survive it," Josh mocked. He looked as though this argument was just getting started, while Willow was acting like it was over. She stormed away, a dirty dish still in her hand.

She didn't look back over her shoulder. She didn't care if he was chasing her or watching her walk away. She was tired. Physically and emotionally spent. Wrongly, she'd believed Josh understood something about her that others were overlooking. He seemed to get who she was and why she was struggling. But his offer to wait for her quickly put that idea to rest.

She swung open the screen door and tossed the dish so hard into the sink it splintered into a dozen pieces. Everyone but Jedda and Crystal had left or gone to bed, and now their eyes were glued on her.

"Where's Josh?" Jedda asked as he stood to grab the broken dish out of the sink and toss it into the trash.

"He's leaving," Willow said as the rumble of Josh's car flooded the kitchen. "He and I didn't exactly agree on why waiting for me to come back to Edenville was a bad idea."

"He offered to wait for you?" Crystal asked, her facial expression looking as though she was in Willow's camp and immediately making her drop her guard slightly.

"Yes. I seriously don't understand how he can't see why that wouldn't work with me."

Jedda's frustration was written all over his face. "You don't like him? Is he not your type? Because he seems like a good guy to me, and he seems to like you, in spite of everything, including your attitude."

"My attitude?" Willow asked full of indignation.

"Jedda," Crystal said, giving him a look to bite his tongue.

"I just don't get it, Willow. I don't understand how you can have the life you've been given and still be unhappy. How you can make the stupid choice to help a guy like Brad and steal from your father. You've had it all. Every opportunity to be happy and still you push everyone away. You run."

Crystal stood between the two of them and raised her hand for Jedda to be quiet. "I don't think you understand where she's coming from and I think you should stop before you say something you'll regret."

"I don't think you get much of a say in this, considering you were only here for one reason. Your own benefit."

Willow watched as Crystal's face went from bold to guilty. She could understand her brother's feelings toward Crystal's actions, but part of her wanted him to get over it. They'd all made mistakes, big ones, but if he didn't let go of this he'd be giving up a damn good chance at happiness.

"If that were true I'd be gone already, so take my advice and give her some space."

"I get that I've been away from the general population for a while and maybe I'm not aware how things work as well as the rest of you, but this seems pretty straight forward. I'm a damned murderer. I was locked up and look at me. I'm trying. I'm taking chances and risks and trying to make better choices. I'm fighting to make this life something I can be happy with and proud of" He stared wearily at Willow. "Can you say the same?"

"I saw you out there," Willow said, softening her face a little. "I saw you make the right choice, as hard as it was for you."

"But?" Jedda asked, begging her with his eyes to explain.

"That isn't where I'm at right now. My being here won't help you. I can't be the person you were hoping to reconnect with. I want you to have a good life and this is the right place for you. You're surrounded by the right people. The best thing I can do for you is leave. It was never my plan to stay anyway. It was only supposed to be a visit. I need to go home."

"Back to that island, hide yourself?" Jedda asked.

"I'll be fine. The best thing you can do right now is let me go."

"I want to know you, Willow. I want to know you better than this. I want to understand you."

"If it makes you feel better, I want to understand me, too." Willow wiped at a rogue tear as it rolled its way down her cheek. "What I do know is I can't have you trying to save me right now. Those days need to be behind me. It's too much for me to carry."

"Too much? Is it that you hate what I did? You can tell me. There is nothing you can say that would hurt me. I just want to know."

"There are times I hate what you did. Then there are times I hate myself for hating you. I feel guilty for hating the person who saved my life. I was given a second chance, all at your expense." Willow looked to the ceiling and blinked back more tears that were forming. "It's an actual weight, like cinderblocks on my shoulders every day. Do you understand what it feels like to know you gave up your freedom so that I could have a chance at life? It's suffocating. Every Christmas present I opened, all I ever thought of was how you'd never get another present. Every horse I rode, every day out in the sunshine on the beach, all my mind did was wander to where you were. What you were doing. I may have tried to look like I enjoyed myself, but in reality all I ever thought of was you and what you lost so that I could have the life I was living. Everything I did was tainted by the idea that you were locked away suffering and doing without." Willow felt her anger growing as she spoke, though that wasn't the emotion she was trying to portray.

"I never had a single regret," Jedda said, as though that would make everything better. "If we were back there right now, I'd do everything exactly the same way."

"I have regrets," Willow whispered, her voice not strong enough to fight her emotions.

Jedda slammed his hand to the table as he let his body fall heavily into a kitchen chair. Crystal reached a hand out to touch him, then drew back as she spoke quietly to him. "Every time you swoop in to help her and risk yourself, it puts a burden on her. If you're playing hero, that automatically makes her the victim. When someone offers to wait for her while she works her stuff out, then she's got that person to worry about while she does it. That's a pressure she doesn't need. When each of us puts our neck on the line for her and stands between her and her problems, all it says is that she's not able to do it on her own. And God forbid something happens to them, then she has to add that to what she's already carrying around."

"Yes," Willow said loudly, her eyes open wide as if she'd just been heard for the first time in her life. "My parents, the people who adopted me, they needed me to feel better, so I felt better for them. You gave up everything for me so that I would have a good life, so I made my life good for you. I got twisted up in what perfection should look like. I couldn't distinguish what I was doing because I thought I should do what you wanted me to do instead of what I wanted to do. Somewhere in the mix of all that, I lost myself. Or maybe I never had a chance to find myself, I don't know. But I know there isn't anything here in Edenville for me. I'll never find myself here."

"I want to fix this," Jedda pleaded. "There has to be a way."

Willow let out an exhausted chuckle as she ran her hands through her long hair. "I know you do. And as long as you think that's your job, I'll always feel this way. I need to stand on my own two feet. I need to figure out who I am when no one is trying to fix me and save me. When no one is expecting me to be perfect all the time. I was stupid enough to think Brad was the answer to that. I thought if I could fit into his world it must mean I'm good enough, I'm healed. I want to fall and fail and screw up without feeling like I've squandered the gifts given to me. I want to feel grateful for what you did and forgive myself for those feelings. I want to live a day without guilt. And that's all possible for me if I know you're here getting your chance at being happy."

"I don't want you to be alone," Jedda choked out, still struggling to understand. "Can this really be what you want?"

"It's what she needs," murmured Crystal, as she locked eyes with Willow. "You have to let her go home, even if it's hard."

Jedda nodded as he stood and wrapped his arms around Willow and rested his chin on the crown of her head. She let her cheek rest on his chest, hiding for one last minute under the strength of his arms. The arms that had saved her, but did not free her.

"You've found your freedom, Jedda. It's right here. You've earned it. I need to go find my own."

"I wanted things to be different between us. To be easy. It used to be you and me against the world. I feel like those days are done for us."

"Just be right here, making sure you're building a life for yourself. Show everyone in this town what kind of person you are and what you can offer. Make them fall in love with you, so that I will always know where to find you. And whatever you do, don't screw things up with her," Willow said, gesturing over to Crystal. "She's brilliant. So work it out."

Willow stepped away from Jedda and headed up the stairs. She was hopeful that he would actually salvage a life out of the cards they'd been dealt. Now she just needed to get out of here and try to do the same for herself.

* * * *

"Did you mean what you said? That you love me?" Jedda asked, still not willing to get too close to Crystal, physically or emotionally.

"I do." She raised her chin adamantly. Her blue eyes seemed like they were in a constant state of near tears since she'd told him about Erica. "It's okay if you don't love me back or if you can't forgive me for what I did. I wanted to be here for the wedding. I felt like that was the right thing, but if you still want me to go now, I will."

"When did it change for you? When was the exact moment you switched from needing something from me to actually caring about me? I feel like I need to hear that from you."

"The moment I realized how much we had in common. It was maybe the third or fourth time I'd visited you in prison and we were talking about your sister. You were telling me what it felt like to see her hurting and how you didn't regret what you'd done for her. I'd do anything for Erica, and I felt like I was finally sitting across from someone who knew what that felt like. I opened my heart up to you that day and I never looked back. A million times I thought about asking you to look at my sister's picture, to know if you had ever seen her. But every time I realized there would be no way for me to do that without you feeling like I'd betrayed you. I was afraid to lose you. Then to lose everyone down here. It all just got away from me."

"I'm sorry about your sister," Jedda said, fidgeting slightly in his chair. "I can't imagine what it must feel like to not know where she is."

"I'm not giving up," Crystal asserted as she straightened in her chair. "I'll never stop looking for her."

"That's admirable," Jedda said as he looked out into the night. "I'm sure it wasn't easy, finding a way to ask me if I'd seen her. I just wish you would have done it earlier."

"Do you want me to go back to New York?" Crystal asked as she nervously tucked her hair behind her ears.

"I don't want to make that decision. Who am I to tell you where you can go and what you can do. Everyone here cares about you. I don't think they want you to leave."

"I honestly only care what you think. Can you forgive me? Can we go back to where we were before all this?"

"Don't ask me that tonight," Jedda said, rubbing the ache out of his shoulder. "I don't want to have to say no to that question. So don't ask yet."

"How will I know when to ask?" Crystal asked as she blinked back her tears.

"You'll know."

Chapter Eighteen

There wasn't much of a goodbye for Willow the next morning. Michael dropped Jules off early while he headed to his office to face Brad's father. The man meant business. Just an hour after Brad left Betty's house, Michael's phone was ringing and an unnamed associate of Brad's father was setting up a face-to-face meeting. He'd taken the red-eye flight and intended to settle all this right away. Bobby went to work, Piper to school. Clay left to work on the restaurant. Willow had said it was what she wanted, everyone just going on with his or her normal routine. Jedda wasn't sure if Josh would show up, and he couldn't read his sister well enough to know if she was disappointed or relieved that he hadn't.

She almost made it to Crystal's car without words of wisdom from Betty. Almost.

"It's okay to leave today. It ain't okay to never come back. You understand?" Betty asked, stroking Willow's long hair. "I know life can be confusing sometimes, but that passes. Just ride it out until it does and make sure you remember you can always come back. I'm sure your parents will be happy to see you. But know that we love you here, too. This door," she pointed behind her to the house, "is always open for you. If you're leaving because you think we're judging the mistakes you made, I'll be happy to set you straight."

"Thanks," Willow said meekly. "That's not why I'm leaving. I know I seem ungrateful, and maybe I've been rude, but I am so appreciative of what you do for people, including my brother. Please take care of him."

"On my honor," Betty promised, crossing her fingers over her heart.

Watching Willow wave as Crystal's car drove off ripped Jedda's guts out. It was too reminiscent of the first time they were separated, shipped off to different foster families. He thought coming out of prison would permanently erase the divide between the two of them. They were both adults, both free, but somehow in spite of all that, he was losing her again. The only peace he had was that she was going back to her parents, heading back to people who loved her.

Betty sidled up to him and rested her small hand on his wide shoulder. "It's impossibly hard watching someone you love so much leave. When they walk right out into the world and there ain't nothing you can do to control them. But she is a bright girl. And she's heading home to her mom and dad. Everything you did here, everything you kept yourself from doing, it shows that you're ready to be out here. You could have killed that boy and hid behind the idea that there was no way around it, but you've grown and you can make better choices. She'll find a way to do the same."

"I would do anything for her," Jedda said, raising his hand to wave his goodbye.

"She knows that. I think she needs to go figure out if she can do anything for herself. She might fall or stumble, but I think she knows if she really needs you, all she's got to do is call."

"What do I do now?" Jedda asked, dropping his hand to his side as the car drove out of sight.

"Clay could use a hand with some of the remodeling at the restaurant tomorrow. You think you'd be up for swinging a hammer?"

"Yes," Jedda smiled. "I've been waiting for a chance to help."

"Also, it's come to my attention that I tend to be a bit presumptuous when it comes to people's feelings. Jules told me I better ask you before I do this. Crystal mentioned she had a degree in business management. Clay and I were going to offer her a job keeping the books at the restaurant. It comes with lodging in the apartment he's finishing today, above the kitchen. Would that be okay with you if we offered it to Crystal?"

"I have no idea," Jedda said. "I guess it depends what hour of the day you ask me. One minute I think I can completely understand what she did and the next I'm blown away that she lied to me, that she kept all this from me. Did she really care about me or was she just trying to get answers about her sister?"

"Why can't it be both of those things?" Betty asked, looping her arm with his. "They sound like they could be completely exclusive explanations. Maybe she started it all for her own selfish reasons, but wouldn't she be gone now if that were the case?"

"I've thought of that. I just don't get why she wouldn't tell me right out of the gate. How can someone look right at you and lie if they really care about you?"

"I'd imagine someone like you could understand how far a person would go for someone you love. But it don't change the question. Do you want her staying here in Edenville, if that's what she wants?"

"I want her to do whatever she wants, while I figure out how I feel."

"You know what might help?" Betty asked as she shot her finger in the air as though she'd just had a revelation. "Dishes. Nothing clears the mind like some scrubbing. I'll get you an apron."

* * * *

The day had dragged on as Jedda tried to pretend he wasn't fighting with himself. The thought of not seeing Willow again for a little while was weighing on him. Her sadness, the small window he'd gotten into her mind, were much darker than he imagined. Her struggle made little sense to him but he knew now he didn't have to understand in order to know it was real.

He wondered how everything turned out today for Michael or what Crystal would say about the job offer. He'd bitten his nails down so low his fingertips ached. He'd run about eight miles through the woods and did so many crunches his abs were still stinging. But none of it was enough to distract him from the waiting. So as the cars began to pull into Betty's driveway, a mix of relief and worry swirled inside him.

First to the porch was Michael. Jules had been upstairs resting most of the day but now made her way to the front door to greet him.

"How are you feeling?" he asked, running his hand across her tired cheek.

"Weird. The baby hasn't been moving much today and I'm exhausted," she said as she stepped onto the porch and Michael helped her settle into her chair. He lifted her feet for her and placed them on the cushioned stool.

"Just take it easy then," he said as Crystal sat down next to her. "Are Bobby and Piper on their way? I want to fill everyone in on how things went with Brad's father. He and his men were in my office all afternoon."

"They're pulling in now," Betty noticed as she handed Jules a glass of water and rested her hand on her daughter's belly for a moment as though she could check on her granddaughter.

Bobby and Piper took their customary seat on the porch swing as Michael began to talk. His voice was weary but not completely defeated, which gave Jedda some hope.

"I met with Thomas Angelo this afternoon and turned over the evidence we had on Brad. I'll tell you what, though, the rumors are completely true, that guy is no joke. He brought a computer forensics team to determine whether or not any copies of the data had been made. When they were satisfied we hadn't copied anything, I was given a stack of papers a mile high. It was a nondisclosure agreement that pretty much stated that if I or Willow ever discuss the evidence against Brad or attempt to form a case against him on this matter we'll be hit with an exorbitant number of fines and face more jail time than Brad would have if he were convicted. I seemed to satisfy all of his terms, and in return he assured me that Brad would have no contact with Willow or any of the people in her life. If he seeks out such contact or attempts to harm her he will be cut off from any family funds and shipped off to a drug rehabilitation center with a military style approach."

"You were convinced he was telling the truth?" Piper asked, clearly still second-guessing the decision they'd all made last night.

"I was looking at a father who knows full well what his son nearly cost him. He doesn't seem to be under any illusions about who Brad is, and he knows the liability that brings to him and his associates. He wants this done as much as we do."

"Brad belongs in jail," Bobby bristled, unable to hold his tongue on the divisive topic.

Michael and Jedda both nodded in agreement. "I know he does," agreed Michael flatly. "And if Willow hadn't done what she did, I think I would have been more inclined to pursue it. But she made her choices."

"Did she tell you why? Did she tell you her side of the story?" Crystal asked hopefully.

"No, she left before telling me." Michael shrugged. "I can't imagine any version of the story that would justify stealing narcotics."

Betty broke in before the debate of right and wrong could go any further. "At least she's on her way home. Maybe some time with her folks will do wonders for her."

"About that," Bobby said, anxiously rubbing his stubble-covered cheek. "She didn't go home. I was worried about her getting out of town safely, since I hadn't heard from Michael yet. I had my partner, Lindsey, follow her to keep an eye out. Willow didn't get on a bus heading north; she got on one heading to the west coast. Lindsey did a force sync on her phone through the bus station Wi-Fi. It was a new phone, she must have tossed her other one, but we can use it to track her as long as she keeps it with her."

"What is Willow thinking?" Jedda massaged his temples. His head felt like it was being crushed by a vice. He'd just come to terms with the idea of his sister leaving, only because he knew she was going back to people who cared about her. But now, the image of her alone on the other side of the country was making it hard for him to catch his breath.

"I don't think she ever planned on going home." Bobby shrugged. "There is one more thing."

"What?" Jedda asked, his hand clutched firmly to the arm of his chair as though he were holding on for dear life. Was Brad following her? Did the police find out about her stealing the drugs and now she'd end up in jail? The worst-case scenarios flashed through his brain.

"She forged her mother's name and cleared out her college bank account. She's got twenty-five thousand dollars with her. I got a call from her parents a little while ago. They've been trying to reach her since the news broke about her connection to Jedda. They didn't even know she was down here. They thought she was still at school. They've been worried sick. They said they had a message on their answering machine from her saying she was all right and very sorry for taking the money, but that she needed some space. She promised to call them soon."

"Call it in," Michael said. "She broke the law by forging her mother's name. Lindsey could get her back here and then, if her mom doesn't want to press charges, at least we'll be able to send her back home. Talk some more sense in to her."

"She's not a child," Crystal argued, a twinge of anger in her voice. "She shouldn't have taken the money, but dragging her home won't solve anything. If you've resolved the Brad issue, if she's safe and Lindsey can tell us where she ends up, then the best thing you can do is let her be. Let her go sing in a club and rent her own place. Let her figure out who she is when no one is there to tell her."

Everyone's eyes were locked on Crystal, and Jedda could almost feel the heat rushing to her flushed cheeks. It wasn't easy being new to this tight knit group and it was even harder to take a different stance on something than they did, but that's what Jedda liked about Crystal. She was brave.

"Crystal's right," he said, not looking over at her. "I want her back here as much as anyone, but forcing her to do it won't work. If Lindsey can tell us where she is then let's give her a little time."

Heads nodded and shoulders shrugged as everyone came to terms with the plan. It wasn't going to be easy to let Willow go, but it was necessary.

Jules leaned forward and the glass in her hand tilted, water splashing to the planks of the porch. "My water," she shouted as she let the glass drop and break.

Betty shot to her feet. "It's okay, dear; I'll get a towel. Don't worry about it. Just a little water."

"No," Jules said clutching her stomach, "my other water." Everyone stood as Jules's words began to sink in.

"You're in labor?" Michael asked as his skin went ghost white. "It's time? This is happening?"

"Either that or I just sprung a damn leak," Jules said as Michael and Jedda helped her to her feet.

Michael's words were coming in a panicked flood. "Where's the bag, the hospital bag, with all the paperwork and the Chap Stick and the coming home outfit? Is it at our house? Should I get it first?"

"Michael," Jules shouted as she latched onto the collar of his shirt and pulled his face down to hers. "Get a hold of yourself or I will leave you here. The bag is in our trunk. Someone get me some dry clothes. Bobby you drive us, because I think Michael needs to put his head between his legs. Ma, you're coming right? I need a backup Lamaze coach in case Nervous Nelly here ends up lying in the bed next to me. Piper, you come too in case Ma drives me crazy and I kick her out. And hurry the hell up, if I have this baby on this porch, I'm gonna be pissed."

Everyone scrambled into motion, bouncing off each other and frantically trying to help. They piled into Michael's car. "I'm gonna be a grandma!" Betty shouted out the window as they pulled away.

Jedda and Crystal were left standing quietly on the porch. How dramatically their lives had changed in the last couple weeks. How fast they both went from being relatively alone, to part of something bigger than they ever imagined. And now here they were alone, wondering what to do next.

Before he could muster up the words he'd been considering saying, Crystal was moving across the porch toward something she'd seen. "What's this?" she asked as she knelt down and picked up a small black jewelry box that lay beneath the porch swing. When Jedda shrugged she flipped it open and saw a beautiful diamond ring. The sun caught the three stones and light glittered across the ceiling of the porch.

"Whose is it?" Crystal asked, searching the box as though someone might have written a name on it. She pulled the ring out and tilted it to the side. "It's engraved," she said, squinting to see the words. "It says, Porch Swing Love."

They both took a second to think and then in unison said, "Bobby and Piper."

Crystal carefully put the ring back into the box and snapped it shut. "She certainly didn't lose the ring while it was in the box. He must have taken it. I bet he was going to propose again." Crystal laughed as she stared down at the stunning ring." We have to take this to them." She pulled her keys from her pocket. "He'll be worried sick that he's lost it and maybe he planned to do this today."

"We can send him a text. Let him know we found it."

"What's the fun in that?"

Chapter Nineteen

As the automatic doors to the hospital whooshed open, Jedda squeezed his hands together tightly. This was his first venture back into the heart of Edenville since Jules kicked a guy for bad-talking her mother and refusing her business because of him. The large box tucked under his arm was feeling like a bad idea now as people began to stare.

"Can I help you with something?" a nurse behind a large desk asked as she glared down at the box with skeptical eyes.

"We're here to see a friend," Crystal said. "Julie Grafton, well actually I guess she's Julie Cooper now. She's having a baby today and we're bringing everyone some lunch while they wait." She pointed down to the box.

"Oh." The nurse seemed to relax a little. "Straight through those double doors and take a left. I'm sure Betty will be happy for something other than hospital food. She was just in the kitchen talking to the staff about overcooking vegetables."

They made their way through the doors, following the signs to the maternity wing and finding everyone gathered in the waiting room.

"Hey," Bobby said, looking eager for a distraction. "Glad you guys decided to come by for the very exciting 'waiting around'."

"We brought lunch," Jedda said, holding up the large box. "Just leftovers from the wedding."

Betty practically ran toward the box as she pulled it quickly from his hands. She shoved the old magazines out of the way to make room on the small coffee table in the waiting room. "I could kiss you two on the lips. I called Clay to come down and bring me something to eat since there isn't a damn thing in this place that could pass for food. He's tied up for another hour, so you two are like angels descending from the heavens."

"With cake." Piper laughed as she sank a fork into the fluffy dessert.

"How is she doing?" Crystal asked as she helped hand out the rest of the food.

Betty filled her plate with some of the barbeque chicken as she gave an update. "She's just about there. On the verge of being fully dilated, and ready to push the last we heard a few minutes ago. They're supposed to call me in there any second," she said quickly, putting her normal manners aside as she shoveled in some food.

"Mrs. Grafton?" a nurse called from behind the reception desk, a phone pressed to her ear. "They're ready for you."

"Oh my word," Betty shouted, and then filled her mouth with more food. She hustled away from the waiting room as she buzzed with excitement.

"I can't believe Jules is about to have a baby," Bobby said, a seriousness falling over his face. "I feel like five minutes ago we were climbing trees and digging for worms."

Piper offered him a bite of her cake, which he gladly took. "I can't believe Michael is about to be a dad. And more than that, I can't believe how fatherly he is now, like overnight he just changed."

"They make a great couple. Just like you two," Crystal said, shooting Jedda a funny look, which reminded him of the ring he had in his pocket.

"Bobby, do you know where the coffee is? I want to get a cup," Jedda asked, shifting his weight nervously from one side to another.

"Yeah, go around the corner—" Bobby started, but Jedda quickly cut him off.

"Can you show me? I don't want to make a wrong turn and end up in a delivery room."

Bobby shrugged and stood up to go with him, though he seemed a bit confused. "It's really not far."

"I know, I was just trying to get you alone," he said in a hushed voice. "Was it too obvious? Do you think Piper suspects anything?"

"I'm starting to suspect something." Bobby shot him a quizzical look. "What's going on?"

Jedda reached into his pocket and pulled the ring box out, resting it in his palm, a big smile on his face. "It must have fallen out of your pocket this morning in all the commotion. Were you planning on giving the proposal another try?"

"No." Bobby grabbed the box hastily and jammed it into his pocket. "I took it off the counter when she was doing dishes and I had it engraved. I just haven't found the right time or the right way to propose again. I didn't want to steal Jules and Michael's thunder, but they kept putting the wedding off. Now with the baby coming I think I should wait," Bobby said in a hushed voice as he looked over his shoulder repeatedly. "I don't want to screw it up again."

"Screw what up again?" Michael asked as he came up behind them, still in the blue scrub shirt he'd been given. "Whatever it is will have to wait while you meet your amazing goddaughter. Because she's ready to see you."

"She's done?" Bobby asked, "I mean, she's here, she's born?"

"Yes," Michael beamed, his smile spreading across his whole face, his eyes lit with pride that Jedda had never seen up close before. Bobby reached into his other pocket and pulled out a handful of cigars. With them, out fell the ring box.

"What's that?" Michael asked, bending down to pick up the box. "Is this Piper's ring?" He flipped it open and clearly already knew the answer to his question.

"No," Bobby lied, "it's a . . . it's something else."

"Shut up," Michael demanded as he rested his hands on Bobby's shoulders. "Are you planning on proposing again? Redeeming yourself?"

"I've been holding onto it for a little while. Just waiting for the right time. I didn't want to take away from everything you and Jules had going on. Piper and I can wait. Let her keep thinking she lost it."

"Bullshit. Let's go. I've got a great idea," Michael said, waving at Jedda to follow along behind him. "If I've learned anything this year it's there is no time like the present. None of us are promised tomorrow and that ring sitting in your pocket is the perfect example." Michael hit the button for the elevator and when the doors opened he pushed Bobby inside.

"Where are we going?" Bobby asked, looking like a deer in the headlights.

"You're coming to meet my daughter. They're moving them both upstairs now. And then you're putting that ring back on Piper's finger. The right way."

Chapter Twenty

Jedda felt too big and very out of place in the small hospital room loaded with joy and celebration. He'd never held a baby before, and if he could help it, he wouldn't break that streak today. Jules looked better than he had expected her to. For some reason he assumed she'd be out cold in her room somewhere alone, not allowed any company. Here she was sitting up, pillows propped behind her, holding her bundled-up baby in her arms and smiling like she'd just won a new car.

"She's so beautiful," Crystal cooed as she leaned over Jules, who drew back the blanket to show her sleeping daughter's face.

"She looks like you, Ma," Jules said as Betty pulled her chair even closer to her daughter's side. "Let's hope she's quieter than you, though."

"Does she have a name yet?" Bobby asked. He and Clay, like Jedda, kept their distance from the fragile package that might get passed around. The women on the other hand looked as though they were ready to form a line.

"She does," Michael said, stroking Jules's hair and smirking at Betty.

Betty raised her chin as she made a declaration. "I've decided it's perfectly fine for you to name her whatever you like. Now that she's here I can see that her name isn't important, she's perfectly perfect in every way. You could call her doorknob and I'd love her."

"Oh, doorknob." Michael snapped his fingers as though he wished he'd thought of that name earlier. "I knew we forgot to go through the inanimate object list when we were picking."

“Her name is Françoise Taylor Cooper,” Jules said as she stared down into her daughter’s angelic face.

“Oh my,” Betty cried, the tears in her eyes spilling over, as Jules handed her daughter carefully to her. “Taylor was your daddy’s middle name.”

“I know,” Jules whispered, her own tears wetting her cheeks.

“We’ll call her Frankie,” Michael said as Jules made room for him on the bed next to her. “I wanted her to have a tough name. If she’s going to have this crazy red hair,” he said as he leaned over Betty’s arms and exposed the crown of his daughter’s head, “then I want to make sure she’s strong enough to win all the fights she starts.”

Betty rocked back and forth as she whispered sweet messages of love into her granddaughter’s ear.

“She’ll be going to get checked out in a few minutes, Ma; let everyone else get a chance to hold her.”

Betty pouted and the men against the far wall all waved their hands in unison that they would not like to ride that ride.

“How about you go see Aunty?” Betty sang in a baby voice as she handed Frankie over to Piper’s open arms.

“Do you know how to swaddle her?” Jules asked Piper as she sat up a little in her bed.

“I read the books, it’s kind of like wrapping a burrito, right?” Piper asked as she laid the baby down on the cushioned changing table.

“Yes. I want her to be warm when they bring her down. Would you take that blanket off and rewrap her?” Jules asked, her smile too big to match the request, prompting Michael to pat her arm slightly to calm her.

"I can try," Piper said, pulling the blanket back and gasping. "It's got marker all over it." Piper inspected the blanket closer looking thoroughly concerned.

"What does it say?" Jules asked, the smile she fought returning.

"It says, 'Aunty Piper, I think you should marry Uncle Bobby,'" Piper read aloud, the words not sinking in, her alarm still focused on the ruined baby blanket. Then suddenly it hit her and her face turned fire engine red. Looped with a few stitches to the side of the blanket was her diamond ring, shining under the fluorescent overhead lights. The ring she thought she'd lost was right there in front of her. "My ring?" she whispered.

Michael stepped forward and pulled the thread, releasing the ring. He handed it to Bobby, then, wrapping Frankie in a new blanket and cradling her in his arms, he settled back down next to Jules. Everyone was looking thoroughly ready to watch the show unfold in front of them.

"Piper," Bobby said as he dropped to one knee and held her hand in his, "I've been carrying this ring around with me, waiting for the perfect moment to do this, and it never seemed to come. I didn't want to screw it up again. Where is the perfect place to ask someone to spend the rest of her life with you? When is the perfect time? Michael reminded me this afternoon that if I stop and wait for everything to be perfect, I'll miss what's right in front of me. You deserve better than me sliding this ring on you while you were doped up after surgery. I can't think of a better time than our goddaughter's birth day, or a better place than this, surrounded by the people who love us, to ask you this question again."

Piper bit hard at her lip and Jedda could see the tremble in her hands. The more time he'd spent around them all, the more he heard about the journey Piper had been on. She'd suffered greatly, faced bleak loneliness, but she'd endured, and here she was. Someone loved her. Actually lots of people loved her. Her life went from empty to full, and maybe his could, too.

He glanced over at Crystal, who had her hands clamped tightly together in nervous anticipation of Piper's answer, and he wanted to go to her. To lace his fingers with hers and experience this moment together.

"Piper Anderson, will you still marry me?" Bobby asked as he slipped the ring onto her finger.

Piper swallowed hard and pulled Bobby up to his feet. "Yes." With a passionate kiss they sealed their future as everyone in the room applauded, then instantly stopped as Frankie let out a loud cry in protest to the noise.

"I think it might be time for her to sleep," Jules said as she handed her back to Betty for some soothing rocking and quiet songs. Everyone began saying their goodbyes and headed for the door.

Before Piper stepped out she looked over at her friend, the new mom who looked perfectly suited for the job. "Do you think it says something about us that we were both proposed to in a hospital room?" Piper asked, leaning in and hugging Jules. "Do you think it's an omen?"

"Yes," Jules giggled, kissing Piper's cheek. "It means we're going to have exciting times, and that we're meant to be in each other's lives."

Michael slapped Bobby's shoulder in congratulations. "Let's make sure we make up a good story for Frankie though. I want her to think we got engaged in a hot air balloon on Valentine's Day," he joked as he waved his goodbye to everyone who was heading for the door.

Jedda caught Crystal's arm and pulled her away from the group and around the corner.

"Ask me again," Jedda said as he stood with his feet planted firmly, his hands rooted on her shoulders.

Crystal's shock turned to a smile, that amazing smile of hers as she began to speak. "Can we go back to the way things were? Can we be friends again?"

"No," Jedda answered, dropping his hands to his side and shaking his head. "We can't."

"So I should go?" Crystal asked, the excitement draining from her body.

"No. You should stay. I don't want to just be your friend. I think I'm in love with you. I was watching you in there and I see the eagerness you have for life and I can't picture not having that around. You're such a positive energy in this world and I naively assumed that was because you hadn't ever been through anything difficult. I figured maybe life hadn't put you through the ringer. Now that I know it has, that you've suffered, but still find a way to shine your light over everyone and everything, it makes me see how incredible you are. I'm much better with you than without you. I want to watch you watch life, because just seeing your openhearted reaction to everything makes me happy."

"I'm so sorry Jedda. I regret terribly what I did." Crystal gulped back her emotions as she brushed fresh tears off her cheeks.

"I forgive you," he said, crouching slightly to align his eyes with hers. "I know what it feels like to want to save someone so badly that you lose yourself in it. You've looked beyond my past and given me a chance. I want to be able to do the same thing with your mistakes. I want you to stay here. Betty's going to offer you a job managing the books at the restaurant. I hope you take it."

"I'm sorry I let my pain blind me. I should have told you sooner." Crystal said as she wrapped her arms around his neck, their smiling mouths just inches from each other. "I won't be reckless with your heart ever again."

He leaned down and kissed her passionately, his arms pulling her in and squeezing her body against his. How had he gotten this lucky? How had he found this much redemption when he felt like he deserved none?

As Crystal leaned back, her wide, ever-present smile staring back at him, Jedda stopped asking himself those questions. The answers didn't matter. The only thing that mattered now was holding onto what he'd been given.

Someone clearing his throat nervously behind them took them both by surprise. Josh stood, his eyes darting uncomfortably around the hallway as Jedda and Crystal stepped apart from each other.

"Hi Josh," Crystal said, straightening her rumpled shirt.

"I just wanted to see how she's doing," Josh said, clearing his throat again.

"She seems okay, the baby was about to go down for a checkup or something," Jedda explained as he pointed over his shoulder back to the room they'd just left.

When Josh didn't answer, his uncomfortable stance growing more so, Crystal seemed to key into what was wrong.

"I don't think that's the she Josh was asking about," Crystal said quietly, touching Jedda's arm gently.

"You mean Willow," he said, his face lighting with understanding. "She left this morning."

"She went back home, back to her parents?"

"No," Jedda responded with a sigh, remember the state Willow had left things in. "She stole a bunch of money out of her college fund and headed out to California. Bobby's partner was watching her when she left and was able to get a good tracking on the new phone Willow picked up. Hopefully she doesn't ditch the phone and we can at least know where she is."

"She's got to have a good reason," Josh said, pushing his hair off his forehead. "I can't imagine she's just running off and stealing stuff for no reason."

"I'm not sure. I keep telling myself I still know who she is, but if I'm honest, she's been out of my life so long, I can't really say I know why she's doing what she's doing." Jedda felt Crystal loop her arm around his and squeeze his tensed bicep.

"If you hear from her, will you tell her that I . . ." Josh hesitated, clearly not sure what message he wanted to pass along. "Just tell her I hope she comes back."

"I will. And If I get a lead on where she is, or find out how she's doing I'll let you know," Jedda said as he grasped Josh's extended hand in a firm shake.

Josh turned on his heels and headed back down the hallway, looking disheartened with his head hung low.

Crystal leaned her head on Jedda's broad shoulder as she spoke, "I think he really cares about her."

"I do too. I just wish she'd wake up and figure out what the hell she's doing."

"At least you'll know where she is. You're lucky to have that, trust me." Crystal's voice was small and tinny as he spun her back into his arms.

"I'll help you. I don't know how, but I'll try to help you find Erica." He leaned down and kissed the top of her head, breathing in her jasmine scented shampoo.

"I think that's what makes us perfect for each other. I know you're never going to give up on Willow and I'm never going to give up on Erica." She rested her head on his chest as he rubbed her back consolingly. She tipped her chin up and smiled into his face brightly. Grasping her cheek firmly he pulled her mouth to his and began to kiss her with a hunger he'd fought off since the moment he'd met her. He backed her slowly to the wall and held her there with the weight of his body, as he continued to kiss her fervently, their tongues clashing with a craving for more.

"I guess you will fit right in with us," Bobby said through a laugh as he rounded the corner.

Piper let out a laugh as Crystal and Jedda split their bodies from each other and tried to right themselves. Jedda wiped at the peach gloss smeared across his lips, Crystal smoothed back her frazzled hair.

"What is it about all of us and hospitals?" Piper asked, shoving Bobby along. "Let's give these lovebirds some privacy. Glad to see you worked it out," she laughed as she winked at them.

"Good choice, bro," Bobby said, slapping Jedda's back on his way by. "But maybe take this party somewhere a little more private."

As they disappeared around the corner Crystal buried her embarrassed face into her hands.

"That sounds like good advice." Jedda leaned his body back against Crystal's. "You still have the keys to your hotel room?" he asked, raising a seductive eyebrow at her.

She slipped her hand into her bag that was still slung across shoulder and fished out the key to the hotel room. She waved it back and forth with a playful smile dancing on her lips.

He looped his hand around her dainty wrist and pulled her along behind him as he raced for the door. They flew past Piper and Bobby, who couldn't contain their amusement. "Drive safely," they called out behind them as Crystal and Jedda stepped outside, the whooshing doors closing out the laughter of their friends.

"They know where we're going," Crystal said with blushed cheeks as she bit at her lip.

"I don't care if the whole world knows." Jedda spun back toward her and scooped her up at the waist, slinging her over his shoulder like a sack of potatoes.

She let out a yelp and a squeal as he spun her around in a circle then dropped her back down to her feet, both of them needing a minute to lean on each other and steady themselves. "You make me happy, Crystal," he said, staring down into her face. "Now let's go see if we can spend the next few hours being really happy." He smiled as he tickled her side then bolted for the car.

Chapter Twenty-One

Little Frankie was the perfect baby, at least according to Betty. If you took one look at her haggardly tired parents you might begin to question that statement.

"Eight-week-olds are supposed to sleep all the time," Michael said as he closed his eyes and rested his head on the dining room table. Apparently a tradition they'd all gotten away from, Betty had revived Wednesday night dinner as a means to make sure everyone took time from their busy schedules to slow down and be together. While they all complained about having too much to do at times, they always showed up.

Tonight's dinner was done and Jules yanked Michael's tired body up from the table. "Come on, we've got a baby to go stare at all night while she stares back at us. I swear this child is nocturnal."

"I told you she just needs a bluebird feather hanging over her door and a rub of some of that ointment I gave you on her belly. It works like a charm," Betty insisted for the fourth time.

"Ma, bird feathers are littered with bacteria and that cream looks like it was made at the turn of the century. How long have you had it?"

"It's been handed down for generations." Betty nodded. "A dab is all you need to get her clock turned back the right way."

"I don't think so, Ma; there aren't any ingredients listed on the bottle. Is it hypoallergenic? Organic? I'm not going to rub it on her."

"It worked for you and you turned out fine," Betty said, reluctantly handing Frankie back to her mother.

"Are you sure you want to make that argument?" Michael asked, gesturing with his eyes over to Jules, suggesting fine was a relative term. He dodged her scornful stare and changed the subject. "Jedda, I've got the information for the counselor over in Ilksville. He comes highly recommended from Josh. I've told him about you and he's ready to meet with you as early as next week. He actually has a great program for transition veterans that he thinks you can benefit from once he alters it a bit."

"Thanks," Jedda said, squeezing Crystal's hand a little tighter. When his nerves flared, having someone to ground him made all the difference.

They all moved out to the porch: Clay with his arm around Betty, Bobby and Piper hand in hand, and Jedda and Crystal leaning together against the railing as they watched Michael fasten in the baby then Jules double check to make sure he'd done it right.

"I passed the bar but two straps and a buckle are too much for me," he jested to everyone on the porch as he waved a final goodbye and they drove off.

Clay and Betty yawned in unison and didn't settle into their rocking chairs, as usual. "We're heading in, kids. The renovations at the restaurant are killing us. We're so close to being finished but we are bushed," Betty said as she blew them all a kiss. "You kids stay out here as long as you like. Jedda just turn everything off when you come in."

"Aren't you guys staying?" Crystal asked as Bobby reached in his pocket for his car keys. "You have to sit there and swing for a little while, it's your thing."

Piper laughed. "Bobby put up a porch swing at our house. It's cute, and we've been sitting on it at night before we go to bed. We're going to head home."

"Good night," Jedda said as he sat on the kitchen chair at the corner of the porch as he usually did.

"We were thinking though," Piper said as she stepped off the porch, "there's no use leaving the thing empty. Someone should swing in it. Maybe it's got a little extra magic in it." She and Bobby hopped in his truck without saying another word.

"You know I believe in magic," Crystal said as she dropped down onto the swing, holding the chain with one hand as she started to move it back and forth.

Jedda raced over and sat next to her, like a little kid getting his turn on an amusement ride. He stared out into the yard, his arm wrapped tightly against Crystal as she leaned against his side.

"What are you thinking about?" she asked as she gently moved the swing along to the rhythm of their heartbeats.

"I'm wondering if I'm wrong to wish Willow was back here. She stole drugs that put people in the hospital, lied about going home, and tricked her parents in order to take their money. Maybe her being gone is a good thing. I think it will make my life less chaotic. But something inside of me just wants her back here. Am I seeing something in her that doesn't exist? And if that's the case, why do I keep hoping she'll pull up here any minute."

"I don't think anyone is completely good or completely bad. Maybe you just came back into her life at a time when she'd made some mistakes. She can come back from them, and when she does, it'll be important for her to know those things don't define her. She can be more than just a culmination of her missteps."

"She was right about one thing," Jedda said as he brushed Crystal's hair to the side. "You are brilliant."

Jedda sighed, turning toward her and bringing his face down to hers. When their lips were only centimeters apart he whispered, "Thank you for believing in me even when I wasn't sure I was worth it. Maybe you're right about magic after all."

"I've converted you? Do you want to go throw a coin in the wishing well?" Crystal asked, lighting with excitement.

"Tomorrow." He pressed his lips to hers and felt the excitement of his love for her run through his body. He always assumed the most intense feelings he'd ever experience were those of rage or fear, but they were like fleeting distant memories compared to the sensations he felt while kissing Crystal.

"I think the swing is working," she joked as he lifted her onto his lap and kissed her even more passionately.

"Then let's never get up," he said, pulling away and locking eyes with her, both his hands bracing her cheeks. "Let's make magic together."

Chapter Twenty-Two

Willow sat in the corner of her nearly empty loft apartment and waited for her phone to ring. She stared down at it and willed it to chime. Finally it cooperated. She juggled it for a moment in her overly anxious hand and then finally put it to her ear.

"Hello?" she said, attempting to make her voice sound stronger than it was.

"Is this Claudia?" the man on the other end of the line asked in a heavy Spanish accent.

"Yes," she lied, her palms soaked with sweat.

"I hear you've been trying to get hold of me for a while. I don't particularly like people who hunt me down. If you got business with me, you better say it now, because after this call you won't hear from me again."

"I'm sorry to have badgered you. I hear you're the guy I need to talk to about setting up a good size score of some new stuff."

"You think I'm dumb enough to talk about this shit on the phone?"

"No, no of course not. I can meet you in person. I have twenty thousand dollars and a proposition for you." The silence on the other end of the phone had Willow pulling it from her ear to check the screen multiple times to see if he'd hung up.

"I'll meet with you tonight. You know where the Saint Charles Bridge is?"

"Yes," she lied again, but was sure she could find it.

"Ten o'clock tonight." She heard the line disconnect and, as she dropped the phone to the table, clutched at her racing heart. She'd done it. She'd actually made contact with the largest distributer of boutique drugs in southern

California and he agreed to meet with her. For a normal drug dealer her measly twenty thousand dollars would be chump change, but Macario Perez was on the ground floor of a completely new industry and he was in need of capital. Or at least that's what Willow had learned since she'd come out here a couple months ago.

This deal was going to be her ticket. Everything she'd planned, all the groundwork she laid, this was going to make it happen. This score was going to finally free her to truly start her life over. She looked down at the backpack full of money that she'd swindled from her parents and felt the knot of guilt tighten in her stomach.

"It's all going to be worth it," she told herself out loud as she stared into the mirror. Her long blonde hair had been cut short and tucked up into a jet-black blunt-cut wig. She had fake piercings trailing up her ears and one in her nose. A prominent henna tattoo was stenciled across her neck and down her chest. None of this suited her much but that was the point. She didn't want to look like herself. When all these pieces she was planning fell into place it would be important that it didn't lead back to her. So the disguise was necessary.

She looked up at the clock and realized it was just after dinnertime back on the east coast. She wondered what her brother would be doing right now. She wondered what they all must think of her running off. Stealing again. Trying to force out those thoughts, she laced up her boots and knotted them tightly. It didn't matter what they thought of her right now because soon enough they'd know the truth. If she could pull this off, then there would be no turning back.

She looked at herself one more time in the mirror before she headed for the door, on her way to finish up some last minute details. Could she really do this? Was this really who she was? Though the answer wasn't completely clear she knew she had to try. She'd come out here for one reason and one reason only—to take Brad down once and for all. She never intended for that deal they made to be the last of the fight she had in her. But the only way to make it happen was to separate herself from everyone else's lives. Two many cooks in the kitchen, Betty would say. This was something she needed to do alone. Not just to protect the people she cared about, but to prove to herself that she could. None of them needed to throw themselves on the sword at her expense. The mistakes she made, the risks she took, were all leading up to this moment.

All she had to do was stand across from a violent drug lord and pitch him a deal he'd likely think was insane. A lump in her throat grew to a suffocating size as she considered what could happen to her.

It was too late now. Her destiny was going to be waiting for her under the Saint Charles Bridge and she was determined to face it. Brad would pay for what he'd done to her, even if she had to go down fighting. All she could hope was when this was over there would still be someone around who loved her.

The End

Follow Willow's story

Settling Scores - May 2014

Sign up for Danielle Stewart's Mailing List

One random newsletter subscriber will be chosen every month in 2014. The chosen subscriber will receive a $25 eGift Card! Sign up today by clicking the link above.

Author Contact
Website: AuthorDanielleStewart.com
Email: AuthorDanielleStewart@Gmail.com
Facebook: Author Danielle Stewart
Twitter: @DStewartAuthor

28291842R00145

Made in the USA
Charleston, SC
07 April 2014